英倫女孩站出來

Elspeth Rawstron 著

安卡斯 譯

ABOUT THIS BOOK

For the Student

🎧 Listen to the story and do some activities on your Audio CD.

🗣 Talk about the story.

Ⓟ Prepare for Cambridge English: Preliminary (PET) for schools

For the Teacher

HELBLING e·ZONE THE EDUCATIONAL PLATFORM A state-of-the-art interactive learning environment with 1000s of free online self-correcting activities for your chosen readers.

Go to our Readers Resource site for information on using readers and downloadable Resource Sheets, photocopiable Worksheets, and Tapescripts. www.helblingreaders.com

For lots of great ideas on using Graded Readers consult Reading Matters, the Teacher's Guide to using Helbling Readers.

Level 5 Structures

Modal verb would	Non-defining relative clauses
I'd love to . . .	Present perfect continuous
Future continuous	Used to / would
Present perfect future	Used to / used to doing
Reported speech / verbs / questions	Second conditional
Past perfect	Expressing wishes and regrets
Defining relative clauses	

Structures from lower levels are also included.

CONTENTS

Hello Elspeth, tell us a little about yourself.

I studied drama at university and then worked for a theater newspaper in London. Later, I decided to train as an English teacher. By a strange twist[1] of fate[2], I found a teaching job in Istanbul in Turkey and I have lived and worked there ever since.

Where do you get your ideas for stories?

The idea for a story often comes when I visit a place. I feel that I'd like to read a story set in that place.

Why did you choose Salts Mill as the location for the story?

Some places make a big impression[3] on you and Salts Mill is one of those places. It used to be a huge old textile[4] mill[5]

but now it's an art gallery. The history of the mill and its owner is fascinating[6]. It's the perfect place for a mystery[7] story.

What is the main theme of the story?

The main theme[8] of the story is children working long hours and in difficult conditions. The characters[9] in the book are fictional[10] but in the past a lot of very young girls like Emily and Grace worked in mills like Salts Mill and a lot of the girls died young. Around the world today, children are still working in dangerous conditions and dying young.

I would like to thank Roger Clarke, an author and local historian[11], for helping me with my research[12] into the historical background of the mill and my mum for taking me there in the first place.

1 twist [twɪst] (n.) 扭轉
2 fate [fet] (n.) 命運
3 impression [ɪmˋprɛʃən] (n.) 印象
4 textile [ˋtɛkstaɪl] (a.) 紡織的
5 mill [mɪl] (n.) 工廠
6 fascinating [ˋfæsn͵etɪŋ] (a.) 極好的
7 mystery [ˋmɪstərɪ] (n.) 神祕事件
8 theme [θim] (n.) 主題
9 character [ˋkærɪktɚ] (n.) 角色
10 fictional [ˋfɪkʃən!] (a.) 虛構的
11 historian [hɪsˋtorɪən] (n.) 歷史學家
12 research [rɪˋsɝtʃ] (n.) 研究

1 At the heart of the story, there is a mystery at a mill. Look at the pictures in the book. Make predictions about the story.

    a What do you think happens? Tick (✓).

        ☐ death   ☐ theft   ☐ murder   ☐ war

        ☐ kidnapping ☐ romance   ☐ ghosts   ☐ business

    b When does the story take place? Tick (✓).

        ☐ in the past   ☐ in the present

        ☐ in the past and the present ☐ in the future

2 There are two stories within the story. Answer the questions using the pictures in the book to help you guess.

    a Which story has the happiest ending?
       The story in the past or the story in the present?

    b How does the story in the past end?
       With a death or with marriage and children?

    c How does the story in the present end?
       With a dream coming true or with a death?

3 Look at the pictures in the book and write the characters' names next to the sentences.

- [a] She works in a mill.
- [b] She goes to school.
- [c] She investigates a mystery in the snow.
- [d] She suffers in the cold but is very courageous.
- [e] She gets into trouble in a shop.
- [f] She has two friends who manage to help her.

4 Part of the story takes place at Salts Mill. Read and complete the text with the words below. Then listen and check your answers.

Salts Mill

polluted   cheaper   better   local   huge
educational   terrible   great   healthier   Industrial

At the time of the (a)............................... Revolution, Bradford was a very (b)............................... city. People lived in (c)............................... conditions and many died young. A mill owner, Sir Titus Salt wanted his workers to live in (d)............................... conditions and have a (e)............................... life, so he built a mill outside the city. It was completed in 1853 and it was called Salts Mill. Sir Titus Salt also built a village with houses for his workers to live in, shops, a church and a park. He later built two schools and a social club and an (f)............................... institute for adults.

The mill continued to produce cloth for another century. In 1976 it was still producing £4 million of cloth a year. At the end of the seventies, a lot of (g)............................... foreign cloth was imported into Britain. Many mills in England lost all their business and had to close. Salts Mill closed in 1986.

In 1987, a 37-year old (h)............................... businessman bought the mill and opened an art gallery, which houses the largest collection of the Bradford-born artist, David Hockney's paintings. There is also a (i)............................... bookshop, an art shop, an interior design shop and a restaurant. Anyone who loves art, books, food or history will fall in love with the mill. It's (j)............................... !

5 Is there a factory, mill or coal mine near where you live? Find out about its history and write a paragraph.

6 Part of the story takes place by a canal. Label the photos of the canal with the words below.

barge   canal   towpath   lock   canal bank

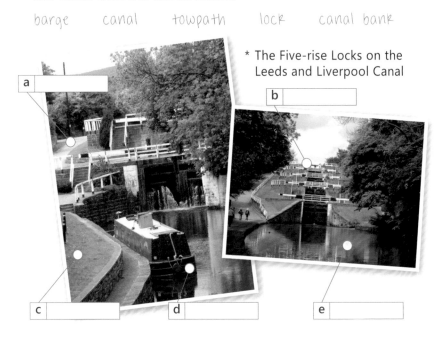

a

* The Five-rise Locks on the Leeds and Liverpool Canal

b

c

d

e

7 Use the words from Exercise 6 to complete these sentences from the story.

a) Then sometimes, my friend Grace and I went for a walk down by the ....

b) We were sitting on the grassy .... when a canal .... went by.

c) It was hard pedaling along the snowy .... by the side of the canal, but Jake was determined.

d) Water poured down on them, but the barge didn't sink, and then it clicked. "It's OK. We're in a .... ," she thought.

8 These verbs are from the story. Match them to their definitions.

_____	a to grip	1	to talk very quietly
_____	b to grab	2	to sew two things together
_____	c to squeal	3	to look at for a long time
_____	d to stitch	4	to talk
_____	e to stare	5	to hold tightly
_____	f to mumble	6	to cry out
_____	g to chat	7	to take quickly
_____	h to slam	8	to shut with force

9 Match these nouns from the story with the pictures.

1) wool   2) lungs   3) leaflets
4) roll of cloth   5) leather book   6) cart

10 Use the words from Exercise 9 to answer these questions.

a Which thing do you think Caterina finds in her grandmother's attic? ....

b Which thing do you think Emily finds by the canal? ....

11 One of the characters, Uncle Sanjit, is a clothes designer who opens a shop. He designs and then produces his own clothes. What do you know about the production of clothes? Put the different processes of clothes production in order. Write the process under the correct picture.

Selling the clothes.
Designing the clothes.
Making the clothes.
Choosing the material to make the clothes.

a

b

c

d

12 Do you like buying clothes? In groups of three discuss what type of clothes you buy and where you buy them from.

13 Where are most of your clothes made? Look at the labels and find out. Do a survey in class and report back to your teacher.

1. The Diary

The year was 1859. Charles Darwin's *On the Origins*[1] *of Species*[2] was published[3]. Big Ben started ticking[4] at the Houses of Parliament in London. Charles Dickens, the famous English writer, published *A Tale of Two Cities*. The Industrial Revolution[5] had by now changed the face of England and my great-great grandmother started working at Salts Mill, a woolen mill in Bradford. She was only eight years old.

> The air was full of a fine white dust that almost choked[6] me. The sound of the machines was deafening[7]. I didn't know whether to cover my eyes or my ears with my hands. I wanted to turn and run but strong hands pushed me into the room. I wanted to scream[8] but no one would hear me.
> I never forgot my first day at Salts Mill.
>
> Emily

The year was 2012 and Caterina was sitting at a table in a corner of the school canteen[9]. It was lunchtime and she could hear the chatter[10] and clatter[11] of plates and knives and forks.

---

1 origin [ˈɔrədʒɪn] (n.) 起源
2 species [ˈspiʃiz] (n.) 物種
3 publish [ˈpʌblɪʃ] (v.) 出版
4 tick [tɪk] (v.) 發滴答聲
5 Industrial Revolution 工業革命
　（18－19 世紀）

6 choke [tʃok] (v.) 窒息
7 deafen [ˈdɛfn̩] (v.) 使聽不見
8 scream [skrim] (v.) 尖叫
9 canteen [kænˈtin] (n.) 學校餐廳
10 chatter [ˈtʃætɚ] (n.) 喋喋不休
11 clatter [ˈklætɚ] (n.) 喧囂

Jake had finished his lunch and he was just about to leave the canteen when he saw her. Her long red hair was pulled back into a ponytail[1]. He couldn't see her eyes but he knew that they were green. She was reading something. Maybe it was the leaflet[2] that everybody was talking about. He had to talk to her about it and now was probably a good time.

Caterina was reading the first paragraphs[3] of the leaflet again when a shadow fell across the table and she heard the chair opposite being pulled out from under the table. Then she looked up and saw Jake. He was tall with dark brown hair and dark brown eyes. Most people said that he was good-looking. He had a nice smile, but right now he wasn't smiling.

"Caterina, what you're doing is unfair[4]," he said. "That's my Uncle Sanjit's shop. He's worked hard for years to save the money to open that shop," he continued.

"Well then, he should be more careful about what he sells in it. The children who make those clothes are younger than you and me," said Caterina defiantly[5], her green eyes flashing[6].

"It's that visit to Salts Mill last month that has upset[7] you, isn't it?" said Jake. "That's OK. We all found it quite upsetting," he continued.

Upsetting

- What has upset you recently?

---

1 ponytail [ˈponɪˌtel] (n.) 馬尾式辮子
2 leaflet [ˈliflɪt] (n.) 傳單
3 paragraph [ˈpærəˌɡræf] (n.) 文章段落
4 unfair [ʌnˈfɛr] (a.) 不公平的
5 defiantly [dɪˈfaɪəntlɪ] (adv.) 大膽對抗地
6 flash [flæʃ] (v.) 閃光
7 upset [ʌpˈsɛt] (v.) 使苦惱（動詞三態：upset; upset; upset）

"No...well, in a way, yes. It's supposed to be history – the workhouses[8] and the child labor. But it isn't history, is it? Who made that scarf[9] you're wearing? How much did you pay for it?"

"A fiver[10]," Jake replied proudly.

"Have you ever asked yourself why it was so cheap?"

"No. And your point is?"

"My point is that some child on the other side of the world is having a horrible life so that you can wear trendy[11] clothes," said Caterina, upset.

"I don't care who made my scarf. All I'm asking is that you don't stand outside my uncle's shop handing out[12] leaflets," said Jake.

"It's too late to stop," said Caterina. "The leaflets are printed."

"But this isn't about a sweatshop[13] in Asia. It's about Bradford. And it's not even about Bradford today. It's about Bradford nearly two centuries ago," said Jake, surprised.

"The first page is about the past but the other pages are about children's lives today," said Caterina.

"What is this?" asked Jake pointing to the first paragraph. "It looks like an extract[14] from a diary or maybe a letter."

"Not exactly," said Caterina. "Emily couldn't read or write. She never went to school." Caterina took an old leather book from her bag and passed it to Jake. "My grandmother died last week," she added.

---

8 workhouse [ˈwɝk͵haʊs] (n.) 工廠
9 scarf [skɑrf] (n.) 圍巾
10 fiver [ˈfaɪvɚ] (n.) 〔英〕五英鎊鈔票
11 trendy [ˈtrɛndɪ] (a.) 新潮的
12 hand out 分發
13 sweatshop [ˈswɛt͵ʃɑp] (n.) 血汗工廠
14 extract [ˈɛkstrækt] (n.) 摘錄

"Oh, I didn't know. I'm sorry," mumbled[1] Jake.

"Well, she did and I found this in her attic[2]."

"So who's Emily?" asked Jake. "She can't be your grandmother. Your grandmother wasn't alive in 1859."

"No, Emily was my great-great grandmother," said Caterina.

"She told my grandmother her life story. Then my grandmother wrote it down for her in this little book. That's where I got the extract from for the leaflet. You can read it if you like. It's very interesting."

"Maybe another time," said Jake, closing the small leather book and pushing it back across the table towards Caterina. "I've got basketball practice now."

Caterina waited for him to get up but he didn't. He was studying her face. "All the girls fancy[3] him," she thought, "but not me. I've got more important things to think about."

Then Jake frowned[4]. "You're really serious about all this, aren't you?"

"Yes," said Caterina. "Yes, I'm really serious about all this."

"My uncle's not going to like it if you ruin[5] his business."

"Yeah, well. Those girls in Asia are not too happy about working seventy hours a week for peanuts[6] to support your uncle's rotten[7] business," Caterina replied.

1 mumble ['mʌmbl̩] (v.) 含糊地說
2 attic ['ætɪk] (n.) 頂樓
3 fancy ['fænsɪ] (v.) 〔英〕愛慕
4 frown [fraʊn] (v.) 皺眉
5 ruin ['rʊɪn] (v.) 毀掉
6 peanut ['pi,nʌt] (n.) 極少的錢
7 rotten ['rɑtn̩] (a.) 腐敗的

Jake was still staring at her and the book was still on the table between them. Caterina could sense[1] people were watching and talking about them. Well, there was nothing to look at or talk about. There was nothing between her and Jake and there never would be.

Jake stood up.

"I'll see you around[2]," he said. Then he was gone. Caterina watched him walk across the room and disappear.

The empty places at her table were soon filled by inquisitive[3] girls. "What did Jake want?" "Did he ask you out?"

"Of course not," said Caterina indignantly[4] and she pushed the leather book into her bag.

She didn't want to show it to anyone else just now. And she certainly didn't know why she had shown it to Jake. "Of course he wasn't interested in it. How stupid of me to show it to him!" she thought.

"What did he want then?" the girls persisted[5].

"If you must know," said Caterina, "he asked me not to stand outside his uncle's shop on Saturday."

"And are you still going to?" asked Helena. Everybody knew about her protest[6] on Saturday.

"Of course I'm still going to," said Caterina and she picked up her bag and walked out of the room.

---

1 sense [sɛns] (v.) 感覺到
2 see you around 回頭見
3 inquisitive [ɪnˈkwɪzətɪv] (a.) 想知道的
4 indignantly [ɪnˈdɪgnəntlɪ] (adv.) 憤慨地
5 persist [pɚˈsɪst] (v.) 堅持說
6 protest [ˈprotɛst] (n.) 抗議
7 throw [θro] (v.) 丟；投（動詞三態：throw, threw, thrown）

8 hoop [hup] (n.) 籃圈
9 pass [pæs] (n.) 傳球
10 slap [slæp] (v.) 拍擊
11 drag [dræg] (v.) 拉
12 What's up? 怎麼回事？（= What's the problem?）
13 get a crush on 迷戀
14 sports hall 體育館

2. Cheap Scarves

Jake threw[7] the ball but he missed the basketball hoop[8]. He couldn't stop thinking about the extract he had read in the leaflet about Emily. Now he wanted to read the rest of Emily's story in the leather book; but he couldn't tell Caterina that, could he? He had never thought about Bradford's past before or how it was connected with the present. It was strange how history repeated and repeated itself. It was strange how events in one country at one point in time could happen in another country at a later point in time. Were no lessons ever learnt?

"Hey, Jake, you missed my pass[9]," said Simon, slapping[10] Jake on the back and dragging[11] his thoughts back to the game. "What's up?[12]"

"Nothing," said Jake. "Look, I'm sorry. I have to go."

"Don't tell me. It's that girl in the canteen, isn't it? Have you got a crush on[13] her or something?"

"No, of course not. It's just there's something I've got to do."

"Can't it wait till after the game?"

"No, it can't." And with that Jake left the sports hall[14].

He heard his team mates shouting at him to stay, but he ignored[1] them. They had a right to be angry, he knew. The team had an important match[2] on Sunday and they needed to train[3] hard. But, he couldn't concentrate[4] on the game; so right now he wasn't any use to them.

He looked at his watch. It was still lunchtime. "Caterina might still be in the canteen," he thought and he ran over there straight away.

It was late and there weren't many students left in the canteen. But Caterina was still there looking through the leather book.

"Thank goodness[5], you're still here," said Jake as he walked over to Caterina.

"What do you want now, Jake?" said Caterina.

"The thing is, I was thinking about your leaflet and I'd really like to read it," said Jake, quickly.

"Are you serious?" said Caterina.

"Totally! I've been thinking about what you said and I'd like to know more." He paused[6]. "My grandfather came here from India to work in one of the factories[7] in the 1950s. Conditions were very different from your great-great grandmother's time but I'm sure they were still hard."

"Yes, but at least he was an adult[8]," said Caterina. "Here, read this and you won't want to buy any more cheap scarves!"

Caterina gave Jake her leaflet and this time he sat down and read it.

1 ignore [ɪgˋnor] (v.) 不理會
2 match [mætʃ] (n.) 比賽
3 train [tren] (v.) 訓練
4 concentrate [ˋkɑnsɛnˏtret] (v.) 集中
5 thank goodness 謝天謝地
6 pause [pɔz] (v.) 暫停
7 factory [ˋfæktərɪ] (n.) 工廠
8 adult [əˋdʌlt] (n.) 成年人

Yes, it's a great T-shirt but do you know the answers to these questions? Where was the cotton[1] picked to make the T-shirt? And more importantly, who picked the cotton? It doesn't tell you on the label[2], does it? But I can tell you.

Child labor is not a thing of the past. Millions of children around the world, from Egypt to India, from Pakistan to Mexico are working long hours to make the clothes you wear.

My name's Aziz and I live in Uzbekistan. Uzbekistan is one of the largest exporters[3] of cotton in the world. Every autumn the schools in my town are shut down and all the students go with their teachers to work in the cotton fields. About a million children, between the ages of five and fourteen, work in the cotton fields. Last year I was sent to a cotton farm far from my home. I stayed in a room with no windows or electricity[4]. We were paid 3 or 4 cents per kilo of cotton. Is it still such a great T-shirt?

My name's Anika.
I'm twelve years old and I live in Bangladesh.
My father and mother both work in a clothes factory.
They don't earn very much so they can't afford[5] to send me to school.
My sister and I have to work in the factory, too. My sister is only nine years old.
Maybe I made the hooded top you're wearing while you were out enjoying yourself with your friends.

That baseball cap[6] looks good, but do you know how many hours I spent sewing caps last year? My name is Parimeeta and I'm twelve years old.
I live in Delhi in India.
My grandmother was sick and she desperately[7] needed money for medicine[8] so she sent me to work. I went to school before but now I work 12 hours a day.

1 cotton [ˈkɑtn̩] (n.) 棉花
2 label [ˈlebl̩] (n.) 標籤
3 exporter [ɪkˈsportɚ] (n.) 出口國
4 electricity [ˌilɛkˈtrɪsətɪ] (n.) 電

5 afford [əˈford] (v.) 供得起
6 cap [kæp] (n.) 無邊便帽
7 desperately [ˈdɛspərɪtlɪ] (adv.) 極度地
8 medicine [ˈmɛdəsn̩] (n.) 醫藥

"OK, you win. I don't want to buy any more cheap scarves, but I still don't want you to stand outside my uncle's shop on Saturday," said Jake. Then he remembered the book. He really wanted to read it but would Caterina still let him?

"You know earlier you said I could read your grandmother's book," said Jake cautiously[1].

"Yes," said Caterina. "And?"

"Well, can I?"

"Sure," said Caterina and she smiled. Then she pulled the little leather book from her bag and gave it to Jake.

As soon as Jake got home that evening, he ran up to his room and took out the little leather book.

As you now know, my name's Emily, and this is my story.

My mother and father grew up in a weaver's[2] village, a few miles outside Bradford, a mill town in the North of England. After my parents got married, they came to Bradford to look for work.

By this time, the Industrial Revolution was in full swing[3]. Bradford was the wool[4] capital[5] of the world, but living conditions[6] were terrible. Often six people lived in one very small room. Black smoke poured from[7] the huge mill chimneys polluting[8] the air. The river was polluted, so there was no clean drinking water. There were frequent outbreaks[9] of typhoid[10] and cholera[11] and life expectancy[12] was very low. Many children died. In fact thirty percent of mill workers' children were dead by the age of fifteen.

Emily

1 cautiously [ˈkɔʃəslɪ] (adv.) 謹慎地
2 weaver [ˈwivɚ] (n.) 織布工
3 in full swing 如火如荼
4 wool [wʊl] (n.) 毛織品；羊毛
5 capital [ˈkæpətļ] (n.) 首都
6 conditions [kənˈdɪʃənz] (n.)（複數形）條件
7 pour from 不斷地大量湧出
8 pollute [pəˈlut] (v.) 污染
9 outbreak [ˈaʊtˌbrek] (n.) 爆發
10 typhoid [ˈtaɪfɔɪd] (n.) 傷寒
11 cholera [ˈkɑlərə] (n.) 霍亂
12 expectancy [ɪkˈspɛktənsɪ] (n.) 期望值

Industry

- Is your town an industrial town?
- Was it an industrial town in the past?
- What did it produce?

My parents were lucky. In 1853, they found work at the new steam-powered[1] woolen mill a few miles outside Bradford. The owner, Titus Salt, wanted his workers to have better living conditions, so he built a whole village around his mill. At first, my parents took the train to work, but later they were given a house in the village of Saltaire, and that's where I spent my teenage years.

My father was an overlooker[2], so our house was bigger than the others. We had a living room, a kitchen and three bedrooms. We even had our own outside lavatory[3] and a small garden. The village was surrounded[4] by countryside and it was a short walk from the house to a canal[5]. We were lucky.

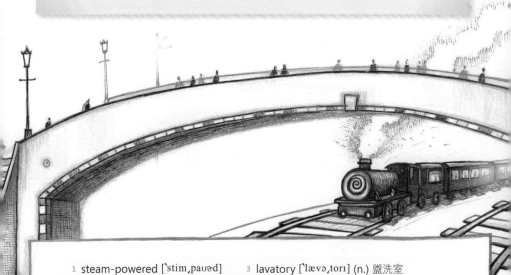

1 steam-powered [ˈstimˌpaʊəd] (a.) 蒸氣發電的
2 overlooker [ˌovəˈlukə] (n.) 工頭
3 lavatory [ˈlævəˌtorɪ] (n.) 盥洗室
4 surround [səˈraʊnd] (v.) 圍繞
5 canal [kəˈnæl] (n.) 運河

27

Family

- Do you know what your grandparents did?
- What about your great-grandparents?
- Where did they live? Find out and share in class.

So now you know where I lived and worked, let's skip a few years.

The year was 1869. Leo Tolstoy, the famous Russian[1] author, wrote *War and Peace* , the vacuum cleaner[2] was invented and the Suez Canal was opened; and I was eighteen years old. The dust from the mill got into my lungs[3] and I had difficulty breathing but so did all my friends. That is, my friends who were still alive — the lucky ones. Lucy died last year. She was sixteen. Katy died the year before that. She was just fourteen. So you see, I was lucky.

But life wasn't all bad. We had fun, too. On Sundays we didn't work. There was the occasional[4] visit to Brown & Muff, the department store in Bradford. Of course we didn't buy anything. We just stared at the magical window displays[5] of ladies' clothes. Clothes we made the cloth[6] for. Clothes we couldn't afford to wear. Then sometimes, my friend Grace and I went for a walk down by the canal.

And it was one cold but sunny Sunday in December, when we overheard[7] the conversation that changed our lives.

We were sitting on the grassy[8] canal bank when a canal barge[9] went by. We could see the barge but nobody on the barge could see us.

---

1 Russian [ˈrʌʃən] (a.) 俄國的
2 vacuum cleaner 吸塵器
3 lung [lʌŋ] (n.) 肺部
4 occasional [əˈkeʒənl] (a.) 偶爾的
5 display [dɪˈsple] (n.) (v.) 展示
6 cloth [klɔθ] (n.) 布

7 overhear [ˌovəˈhɪr] (v.) 無意中聽到 (動詞
　 三態：overhear; overheard; overheard)
8 grassy [ˈɡræsɪ] (a.) 長滿草的
9 barge [bɑrdʒ] (n.) 大型平底船；駁船
10 steer [stɪr] (v.) 掌舵
11 cart [kɑrt] (n.) 手推車

There was nothing unusual about the two men steering[10] the barge. What was unusual was that the barge stopped.

"This is the place, Harry," said the tall man with the red hair.

"Are you sure about this?" asked his friend.

"Yes, there's an old cart[11] in the field over there. We can leave it under that until we come back tonight."

They carried a heavy-looking object[12], wrapped[13] in some old sacks[14], off the barge.

"What do you think it is?" whispered Grace and she gripped[15] my arm tightly.

"It looks like a dead body," I said and she squealed[16].

The men stopped.

"What was that?" asked the man called Harry.

"I don't know," said the red-haired man. "Maybe there's somebody up there behind those bushes[17]. I think we should go and take a look."

Grace went white and we stared at each other in terror[18]. Then a cat leapt[19] out from under a bush and ran towards the men.

"Hey, Harry, it's nothing to worry about. It's just a cat. Let's get on with[20] the job."

---

12 object [ˋɑbdʒɪkt] (n.) 物體
13 wrap [ræp] (v.) 包裹
14 sack [sæk] (n.) 粗布袋
15 grip [grɪp] (v.) (n.) 緊握
16 squeal [skwil] (v.) 發出長而尖的叫聲

17 bush [buʃ] (n.) 灌木叢
18 terror [ˋtɛrɚ] (n.) 恐怖；驚駭
19 leap [lip] (v.) 跳躍（動詞三態：leap; leaped, leapt; leaped, leapt）
20 get on with 馬上進行……

"Jake, dinner time," his mum called up the stairs.

"OK," Jake shouted back.

Bother[1]! The story had just started to get interesting and he wanted to carry on[2] reading. Why did meals[3] always have to be at the most inconvenient[4] times?

Interesting

- Why has Emily's story started to get interesting?
- Are you sometimes interrupted while you are reading an interesting story?
- What makes a story interesting?

When Jake walked into the dining room, everybody was sitting round the table. They all stopped talking when he walked in.

"Oh, no! What have I done now?" he thought.

Then he saw his uncle.

1 bother ['bɑðɚ] (int.) 真麻煩
2 carry on 繼續
3 meal [mil] (n.) 一餐
4 inconvenient [,ɪnkən'vinjənt] (a.) 不方便的
5 sink [sɪŋk] (v.) 下沉（動詞三態：sink; sank/sunk; sunk/sunken）
6 stitch [stɪtʃ] (v.) 縫
7 assure [ə'ʃur] (v.) 確保
8 material [mə'tɪrɪəl] (n.) 原料
9 respectable [rɪ'spɛktəbļ] (a.) 好名聲的
10 supplier [sə'plaɪɚ] (n.) 供應商

4. Jake

 "Sit down, Jake," said his father. "We'll eat dinner first and then your uncle has something he wants to talk to you about."

After dinner, his brother and sister went to do the washing up. Uncle Sanjit pulled a leaflet out of his pocket and put it on the table.

Jake's heart sank[5]. It was Caterina's leaflet.

"It's nothing to do with me," said Jake.

"I know," said his uncle, "but I want you to stop this protest on Saturday. Can you talk to the girl? She's at your school, isn't she?"

"Yes and I've already tried to stop her but she won't listen to me."

"Maybe you could just try and talk to her one more time. You know how much this shop means to me," said Uncle Sanjit. "These children in the leaflet – they haven't made the clothes in my shop."

"How do you know that?" asked Jake.

"Because all the clothes in my shop are produced here in Bradford. The business is run by an old friend of mine. And I know every one of the people who stitch[6] my clothes and I can assure[7] you that not one of them is younger than you."

"And where did you get the material[8] from?" asked Jake.

"From a respectable[9] supplier[10] in London," replied his uncle.

"And where was the cotton for that material picked?"

Now his uncle looked unsure of himself. "I don't know, Jake." There was another pause.

"Look, if it's really important to you, I'll ask the suppliers. They're coming up from London this evening."

"Cool," said Jake. "Then I'll ask Caterina to call off[1] the protest, but I can't promise anything."

"Thanks, Jake," said Uncle Sanjit and he got up to leave. Then he sat down again. "On second thoughts, why don't you call Caterina now? I don't want to leave anything to chance[2]. I've waited a long time to open this shop."

"I'm not sure if she'll come, Uncle," mumbled Jake.

"Well, call and find out," said Uncle Sanjit. "Come on. Jump to it[3]. We haven't got all night."

Jake took out his phone and texted Caterina.

My uncle's here now. Come and meet him. He'll explain everything.

Fab[4]. What's your address?

2 Princess Street ☺

Caterina already knew the address but she didn't want Jake to know that. Quickly, she turned off her laptop[5] and grabbed[6] her coat.

"I'm going to Samira's," she called to her mum.

"Don't be late," her mum called back as the door slammed[7] shut.

Contact
- How do you normally contact your friends?
- Texts/Twitter/Facebook/phone/email/letter?

5. Uncle Sanjit

  It was only when Caterina stood on the doorstep that she began to feel nervous. Nervous about what? About confronting[8] Jake's uncle or about seeing Jake? About confronting Jake's uncle, of course. No, that wasn't true. Caterina was never afraid of confrontation. In fact she loved it. The truth was, she was nervous about seeing Jake.

She pressed[9] her finger on the doorbell – 5, 4, 3, 2 – the door opened and there was Jake.

---

1 call off 取消
2 Don't leave anything to chance.
　做事情不要憑運氣。
3 jump to it 趕快
4 fab [fæb] (a.) 〔口〕太好了

5 laptop [ˈlæptɑp] (n.) 筆電
6 grab [ɡræb] (v.) 抓取
7 slam [slæm] (v.) 猛地關上
8 confront [kənˈfrʌnt] (v.) 使面對
9 press [prɛs] (v.) 按壓

"That was quick," he said.

"Yeah, well I only live two streets away," Caterina replied.

"Really? I never knew that," said Jake. But Jake did.

He knew a lot about her and he knew where she lived. He just didn't want Caterina to know that.

"Are we going to stand here all night or are you going to invite me in?" asked Caterina.

Jake smiled and stood aside. "Don't be too hard on him," he said quietly so only she could hear. "He's alright, my uncle."

Jake's uncle was sitting at one end of a long dining table with a pile[1] of Caterina's leaflets in front of him.

"Uncle, this is Caterina. Caterina, this is my uncle Sanjit."

"Sit down," said Uncle Sanjit. "You know, if you weren't trying to close me down, I'd employ[2] you! You've got real talent[3]," he said.

"You're making money out of children," said Caterina.

"You don't know that," said Uncle Sanjit calmly. "Hear me out[4] first. Don't jump to conclusions[5]."

Then he explained everything about the business, just as he had explained to Jake.

"So," said Caterina triumphantly[6], "you don't know if children are employed in the production of your clothes or not. Did you read this?" she asked, pointing to the passage[7] in her leaflet about cotton picking in Uzbekistan:

---

1 pile [paɪl] (n.) 堆
2 employ [ɪmˋplɔɪ] (v.) 雇用
3 talent [ˋtælənt] (n.) 才華
4 Hear me out. 聽我把話說完。

5 jump to conclusions 急著下結論
6 triumphantly [traɪˋʌmfəntlɪ] (adv.)
   得意洋洋地
7 passage [ˋpæsɪdʒ] (n.) 一段（文章）

"The government of Uzbekistan said, 'Children are not allowed to pick cotton in this country.' But *Newsnight* filmed[8] a field full of children picking cotton. One boy told *Newsnight*, "I won't go to school until November. I pick seventy kilos of cotton here a day." Another boy said, "I'm paid two pence[9] a kilo." Some of the children were as young as nine. Cotton..."

"Yes, I see your point," interrupted Uncle Sanjit, "and I agree with you. Child labor is a terrible thing. I'll talk to my suppliers about it this evening. I promise. Now Caterina, tell me. What do you want to do when you leave school?"

"Me?" asked Caterina. "I want to go to the London School of Economics[10]. I'm going to study politics[11] and then I'm going to be a politician[12] and stop things like this from happening."

---

8 film [fɪlm] (v.) 拍影片
9 pence [pɛns] (n.) penny
   （便士）的複數

10 economics [ˌikəˋnɑmɪks] (n.) 經濟學
11 politics [ˋpɑlətɪks] (n.) 政治學
12 politician [ˌpɑləˋtɪʃən] (n.) 政治家

"I see," said Uncle Sanjit. "You've got big dreams and I hope one day they'll come true for you. "Aim[1] high," my father always used to say. "You don't want to end up[2] like me working in a mill all your life." And he was right. I didn't. I wanted to open a shop and sell good quality clothes at affordable[3] prices. I wanted to employ my friends and most importantly of all, I wanted to design[4] the clothes myself."

"And did you design the clothes?" asked Caterina.

"Yes, I did," replied Uncle Sanjit. "And I hope you'll come to the shop on Saturday and see them. And maybe even like them. You see, Caterina. This shop was my dream. And I'm so close to realizing[5] it," he said. "Don't stop me now."

Big Dreams

- What do you want to do when you leave school? Discuss with a partner and then tell the class.

"I won't stop you if your suppliers can guarantee[6] that their cotton comes from a good source[7]," said Caterina.

"Yes," said Uncle Sanjit. "Well, that will be the first thing that I ask them then." Then he looked at his watch. "I have to go. The suppliers will be arriving at the station in twenty minutes."

"Are you going to take them to the shop?" asked Caterina.

---

1 aim [em] (v.) 瞄準（目標）
2 end up 以⋯⋯作收場
3 affordable [əˋfɔrdəbl] (a.) 買得起的
4 design [dɪˋzaɪn] (v.) 設計
5 realize [ˋrɪəˌlaɪz] (v.) 實現
6 guarantee [ˌgærənˋti] (v.) 保證
7 source [sors] (n.) 來源

"Yes, we'll have the meeting in the shop. They're staying in the flat above the shop tonight."

"Well, good luck then," said Caterina.

And in that second, she knew that she wanted to go to the shop, too. She needed to be at that meeting. She needed to hear what the suppliers said herself. She pushed her chair back and stood up.

"I have to go," she said to Jake.

"Stay if you want," he said.

"No, I have to go. I promised I wouldn't be late."

"OK. See you at school tomorrow then," he said trying not to look disappointed[1].

"Yeah, see you at school," said Caterina.

Uncle Sanjit and Caterina left the house together.

"I'll give you a lift home[2] in the car, if you like." said Uncle Sanjit.

"No, it's OK. I'll walk. I live just round the corner," replied Caterina.

And so they went their separate[3] ways. Each of them was thinking about the meeting with the suppliers. Each of them was thinking about children working long hours in factories and about cotton fields in faraway[4] countries.

Why is it that some children, who should be enjoying their youth and preparing for their futures, are denied[5] the dreams of Caterina and Uncle Sanjit?

---

1 disappointed [ˌdɪsəˈpɔɪntɪd] (a.) 失望的
2 give sb a lift home 順道載某人回家
3 separate [ˈsɛpəˌret] (a.) 個別的
4 faraway [ˈfɑrəˈwe] (a.) 遙遠的
5 deny [dɪˈnaɪ] (v.) 否認；拒絕給予
6 body-shaped [ˈbɑdɪˌʃept] (a.) 人形的
7 package [ˈpækɪdʒ] (n.) 一包東西
8 place [ples] (v.) 放置

6. The Package

The door closed behind Caterina and Uncle Sanjit. It was seven o'clock – too late to go and train with the basketball team now. Besides, it had just started to snow. Then Jake remembered the book. He went up the stairs two at a time and threw himself onto the bed. He picked up the little leather book and carefully turned the pages until he came to the right place in the story.

"Hey, Harry, it's nothing to worry about. It's just a cat. Let's get on with the job."

Then the two men walked across the field towards the old cart, carrying the long body-shaped[6] package[7]. Grace and I watched them place[8] the package under the cart and then we watched them walk away.

"Let's go and see what's in the package," I said, and stood up. My friend, Grace, pulled me down again.

"Are you mad[1]?" she whispered loudly in my ear. "Wait until we're *sure* they've gone. Look, I think I recognize[2] one of the men."

"Which one?" I asked.

"The tall man with the red hair. He works with my father. They load[3] the bales[4] of cloth onto the barges," said Grace.

"Maybe that's not *all* they load onto the barges," I said.

"What do you mean?" asked Grace.

"Dead bodies," I said.

"Don't be silly," said Grace and she shivered[5]. "You're scaring[6] me."

Their voices drifted[7] across the field towards us and we caught some of their conversation. "...here tonight...will pay us two shillings[8]."

"They're coming again tonight," I whispered excitedly.

Then we watched the two men walk up through the field and climb over the wall at the top.

"Come on. They've gone now. Let's go and see what it is," I said and held my hand out to Grace. Grace took my hand and I pulled her to her feet[9].

"I'll race[10] you there," I said and I ran off.

"Don't run," said Grace. "You know what happens when you run."

---

1 mad [mæd] (a.) 發瘋的
2 recognize [ˈrɛkəɡˌnaɪz] (v.) 認出
3 load [lod] (v.) 裝載
4 bale [bel] (n.) 大捆；大包
5 shiver [ˈʃɪvɚ] (v.) 發抖
6 scare [skɛr] (v.) 使驚嚇
7 drift [drɪft] (v.) 漂流

8 shilling [ˈʃɪlɪŋ] (n.) 先令（英國的銀幣名）
9 put sb to one's feet 使某人站穩
10 race [res] (v.) 賽跑
11 solve [sɑlv] (v.) 解答；解決
12 slow coach 用來形容某人慢吞吞的
13 string [strɪŋ] (n.) 線；細繩
14 a roll of 一捆……

I knew. But I didn't stop running. The sun was shining and there was a mystery to be solved[11]. I didn't want to think about my illness that day. I got to the old cart and there was the package. I wanted to pull the old sacks off the package but something stopped me. I sat and waited for Grace.

"Come on, slow coach[12]! Hurry up!" I called excitedly.

Grace walked over to the cart and kneeled down beside me.

"Are you ready?" I asked.

"Yes," said Grace.

Carefully I untied the string[13] around the package. Then, together we pulled the sacks off. There wasn't a dead body inside. There was just a roll of[14] cloth. And we both recognized the cloth. It was from Salts Mill.

"They're stealing cloth from the mill," I said shocked.

"We have to tell someone," said Grace.

"Yes," I said, "but not yet. We'll come back tonight. We'll see who they meet."

"I don't want to come back tonight," said Grace.

"Then I'll come by myself," I said. I wasn't afraid of the dark.

When you worked in a mill, you were afraid of the machines and you were afraid of the overlooker. They were far more terrifying[1] than the darkness. I loved the silence of night-time. And in fact, I loved the darkness because with the darkness came the end of the working day.

So that night, I walked back to the canal alone. It was a clear night and I could see the stars. I hid in some bushes near the cart, and waited.

I didn't have to wait for long. First, the man with red hair came. He stood by the old cart and coughed, a horrible chesty cough[2] that broke the silence of the night. Then along came another man. I recognized him and my heart sank. It was Grace's father.

"Poor Grace," I thought. "I can't tell anyone about this. Grace's father will go to prison[3]. The family will lose their house. Grace will lose her job. They'll have no money and no home. They'll die."

I looked into the darkness for an answer. "I have to tell someone," I thought. And there was only one person I could tell. There was only one person I could trust. That was James.

James' father was an important overlooker. "The overlooker won't believe me. But maybe he'll believe his son. James loves me. He'll listen to me."

---

1 terrifying [ˈtɛrəˌfaɪɪŋ] (a.) 令人害怕的
2 chesty cough 痰咳（帶痰的咳嗽，非乾咳）
3 prison [ˈprɪzn̩] (n.) 監獄

The two men shook[1] hands. Grace's father picked up the roll of cloth. "I got five shillings for the last roll. That's a month's wages[2]. Here's your cut[3]." He handed the red-haired man two shillings.

"Same time next week," he called and then walked off into the night.

The red-haired man leant[4] against the old cart for a few minutes, coughing. Then he walked off in the opposite[5] direction.

I waited a few minutes and then I ran home.

⁂ ⁂ ⁂ ⁂ ⁂ ⁂ ⁂ ⁂ ⁂ ⁂

The next morning, the knocker-up[6] tapped[7] on the window and we all got up. It was 5.30 and it was still dark. We got dressed quickly and ran outside to join the stream[8] of workers going to the mill. We didn't have breakfast. There was a break for breakfast at 8.30.

As usual, Grace and I walked to the mill together. This was the one time in the day when we could chat.

---

1 shake [ʃek] (v.) 握（手）（動詞三態：shake; shook; shaken）
2 wage [wedʒ] (n.) 薪水
3 cut [kʌt] (v.) （分到的）一份
4 lean [lin] (v.) 倚；靠（動詞三態：lean; leaned, leant; leaned, leant）
5 opposite [ˈɑpəzɪt] (a.) 相反的
6 knocker-up [ˈnɑkəˌʌp] (n.) 叫人起床上工的人
7 tap [tæp] (v.) 輕敲
8 stream [strim] (n.) 人潮

"What happened?" asked Grace in an excited voice. "Did you go?"

"Yes," I said. "They're stealing the cloth and selling it."

"Really!" said Grace, shocked. "I'm going to tell my father."

"No, don't," I said and I gripped[1] Grace's wrist.[2]

"Ouch! You're hurting me," said Grace.

"Sorry," I said. "But you mustn't tell anyone, especially not your father."

"But why not? That man's my father's friend," said Grace.

"That's why you shouldn't tell him anything. It will upset him and you don't want to do that," I said.

"No," said Grace.

Grace didn't want to upset her father. He was a wonderful father and she loved him. He wanted the best for his children. And even though he had no money, he always bought them little treats[3].

The bell rang. It was 6 o'clock and the mill was open.

Emily

- Do you think Emily does the right thing?
- What would you do?

1 grip [grɪp] (v.) 緊握   4 assume [ə'sjum] (v.) 假定
2 wrist [rɪst] (n.) 手腕   5 drawer ['drɔ] (n.) 抽屜
3 little treats 小禮物   6 notepad ['notpæd] (n.) 筆記本

7. Caterina

A thought came to Jake and he stopped reading – Uncle Sanjit hadn't asked him what he wanted to do when he left school. No one asked him. They all just assumed[4] that he wanted to be a basketball player. But he didn't. Yes, he was a good player and yes, he loved basketball but that wasn't the only thing he loved.

Jake got off the bed and went to his desk. He pulled open the top drawer[5] and took out a notepad[6] and pen. He loved drawing. He didn't want to be a basketball player. He wanted to be an artist. I mean who was cooler: David Hockney or David Beckham? It was strange how most people his age thought that sport was cooler than art.

Jake wanted to go to art college. He was sure of that. He picked up the pen and started to draw. He drew the mill and he drew the girls leaving the mill, climbing the stone steps to Victoria Road above. One girl turned to face the reader. That was Emily. Only it wasn't Emily. Her face was familiar. It was Caterina's face. He was drawing Caterina.

"Where is Caterina, now?" he thought.
'What is she doing?"
He wanted to text her.
Should he text her? Why not?
Message sent. No regrets. Not yet anyway.

Caterina was walking to the bus stop. It was now snowing.

"The falling snow is white like cotton balls, the cotton balls picked by children in Uzbekistan – maybe it's a sign[1]," thought Caterina and pulled her coat up around her ears. She didn't really believe in signs. Samira did though. "Samira would tell me what the sign meant," thought Caterina and she smiled.

It was very cold. Caterina stood at the bus stop and waited. The snow was falling thick and fast[2] now. The bus arrived and she got on. It moved off and slowly made its way into the town center.

"Don't stay out too late," said the bus driver as she got off. "If it carries on snowing like this, there won't be any buses later."

The snow was covering the ground so Caterina slid[3] down the street passed the Kirkgate Center. Down past the Wool Exchange and across Market Street to where the old Brown & Muff department store had been until the late 1970s. This was Uncle Sanjit's new shop. Of course, it was different now but the building was the same.

Uncle Sanjit had explained to Jake and Caterina earlier that he used to come here as a child with his mother. All the other children looked at the toys, but Sanjit always looked at the clothes.

Uncle Sanjit grew up in the 1970s, so the clothes he looked at in the window displays were stripy[4] catsuits[5], purple flared trousers[6], platform shoes[7]... At the time it was all so new and so colorful.

Back in the 1970s the LCD[8] (Liquid Crystal Display) screen and floppy disk[9] were invented. Skylab[10] 3 carried the first fish and spiders into space[11]. ABBA had their first UK hit single with "Waterloo". The Bay City Rollers were pop idols[12], and *Starsky and Hutch* was a popular TV show. The film *Grease* was a box office[13] hit[14] at the cinema. Pink Floyd had a number one hit with "Another Brick in the Wall", and the disco diva[15], Gloria Gaynor recorded her hit single "I Will Survive[16]".

1 sign [saɪn] (n.) 徵兆
2 thick and fast 大量而急速地；密集地
3 slide [slaɪd] (v.) 滑（動詞三態：slide; slid; slid）
4 stripy [ˋstraɪpɪ] (a.) 條紋狀的
5 catsuit [ˋkætsut] (n.) 全身緊身衣；連衣褲裝
6 flared trousers 喇叭褲
7 platform shoes 矮子樂鞋
8 LCD 液晶顯示
9 floppy disk 磁碟片
10 Skylab（美國 NASA）天空實驗室
11 space [spes] (n.) 太空
12 pop idol 流行偶像
13 box office 電影票房
14 hit [hɪt] (n.) 熱門的事物
15 diva [ˋdivə] (n.) 天后
16 survive [səˋvaɪv] (v.) 活下來

Those were the 1970s and Uncle Sanjit had had a dream. He wanted to be a famous fashion designer[1].

Then, Uncle Sanjit went to Saint Martins College in London to study fashion. Brown & Muff was closed down, too.

For years, the department store stood empty, a dusty building full of two centuries of memories. But every time Uncle Sanjit walked by, he imagined it filled with[2] shoppers, admiring[3] *his* designs.

He imagined children stopping to stare at the wonderful window displays, and he imagined mothers finding just what they'd been looking for, for Britney or Jade, for Ali or Natasha or for Jamila or Abida. Brown & Muff had closed a long time ago but Caterina's mother often talked about it, too.

1970s

- What other things do you know about the 1970s? Work in pairs. Use the Internet to help you.

Caterina stood in front of it now, and she stared up at the new shop sign Boho Chic[4]. Everybody was excited about the opening of this shop. *Be Chic on the Cheap. Look Cool for Next to Nothing.*

The window displays were hidden behind brown paper[5]. It had been like that for weeks. Everybody wanted to see what lay behind the plain[6] brown paper.

1 fashion designer 服裝設計師
2 fill with 充滿……
3 admire [əd`maɪr] (v.) 欣賞；誇獎
4 Boho Chic 波希米亞風
5 brown paper 牛皮紙
6 plain [plen] (a.) 素面的

8. Boho Chic

Caterina saw a car park on the other side of the street.

"It must be Uncle Sanjit and the suppliers," she thought.

Quickly she turned to face the shop window. She listened to the voices that were muffled[1] by the snow and she heard the key turn in the lock. Then the voices faded[2] to silence – just her and the snow now.

She waited a few minutes. Then she went to try the door.

"Phew[3]. It's open," she thought and slipped[4] inside.

It was dark, but there was a light on in a room at the far end of the shop. Caterina walked quietly towards it. She chose a clothes rail[5] near the office to hide behind. And from her hiding place, she could hear everything the men said. Their voices echoed[6] loud and clear around the store.

"The cotton – why do you want to know where it was picked? Does it really matter?" asked Sid, one of the suppliers.

"Yes, it does," said Uncle Sanjit. "I don't want to use cotton picked by children. Now tell me where you bought the cotton or the deal's off[7]."

"But you like our material. It's good quality and it's a good price," said Aamir.

"Yes, yes, I know. But please tell me where you bought the cotton," insisted Uncle Sanjit.

"India, of course," said Sid suddenly[8]. "We always buy our cotton from a small cotton farm in India. We've visited it a few times and we can assure you that there are no children working there. The living conditions of the workers are very good. You're welcome to come and see for yourself. We can go there together if you like."

"Yes, one day I will come and visit the cotton fields with you," said Uncle Sanjit. "That's a relief[9]. I just need to know that the cotton isn't picked by children."

"We understand," said Sid. "Now if that's all, I think you should go, Sanjit. It's snowing quite heavily out there."

"Yes, you're right," said Uncle Sanjit. "Now here's the key to the flat[10] upstairs. I think you'll find everything you need up there. Oh and I'll leave the car here. I don't fancy[11] driving on a night like this. I'll walk; it's not far. I'll leave the car keys with you, just in case[12] you need to move the car. We'll walk to the bank from here in the morning. I'll come for you about nine."

"Okay, we'll see you first thing in the morning."

"Good night then," said Uncle Sanjit.

Then Caterina watched as he left the shop.

---

1 muffle [ˋmʌfl] (v.) 蒙住（以減其聲）
2 fade [fed] (v.) 聲音變微弱
3 phew [fju] (int.) 呸！啐！
4 slip [slɪp] (v.) 滑行
5 rail [rel] (n.) 欄杆
6 echo [ˋɛko] (v.) 回聲；回響
7 off [ɔf] (a.) 失效的
8 suddenly [ˋsʌdnlɪ] (adv.) 突然地
9 relief [rɪˋlif] (n.) 寬心
10 flat [flæt] (n.) 〔英〕公寓
11 fancy [ˋfænsɪ] (v.) 喜歡；想要
12 in case 假使

"You lied to Sanjit," said Aamir, the other supplier.

"So what?" said Sid. "He's happy. We're happy. Everyone's happy. He doesn't need to know the cotton was picked in Uzbekistan."

"Oh, no!" thought Caterina. "Poor Uncle Sanjit. How dare[1] these men lie to him like that! What am I going to do now? I can't call the protest off now. The cotton most probably[2] was picked by children."

Ting ting went Caterina's phone. It was Jake's message. *Ting ting*, loud and clear – it echoed around the shop sounding like a fire alarm rather than a mobile phone. "Oh, no," thought Caterina.

'Why didn't I switch my phone off?"

"What was that?" asked Aamir.

"It sounded like a mobile phone to me," said Sid. "There's someone in the shop."

Sid ran out of the office. Caterina ran towards the main door but she wasn't fast enough. Sid threw himself at her legs and pulled her to the floor. Her head hit the floor. "Ouch," thought Caterina and that was her last thought before everything went black and the pain in her head stopped.

"We can't leave her here," said Aamir in a panic[3]. "She's hurt."

"We can't let her go," said Sid. "She heard everything. She'll tell Sanjit and he'll call the deal off. We need to keep her somewhere. Come on, Aamir. You're from round here. Where can we hide her?"

"Alright, alright. I'm thinking," said Aamir.

A clock ticked somewhere in the shop, tick, tick, tick, tick – the ticking made him nervous. He couldn't think straight. Tick, tick but then he remembered his uncle's old barge.

"I've got an idea," said Aamir.

---

1 dare [dɛr] (aux.) (v.) 竟敢
2 most probably 很有可能；八成
3 panic [ˈpænɪk] (n.) 恐慌

9. Trouble

Jake continued reading the diary. He really wanted to know how Emily's story ended.

James and I wanted to get married. And then we wanted to run away — far away from the mill and the dust and the noise, the tiredness and the sore[1] bones and the terrible coughs.

We planned to find a small cottage[2], maybe in the Lake District. Someone told us it was pretty up there. We wanted to grow[3] vegetables and keep[4] sheep. I wanted to spin[5] wool like my grandmother did. We wanted to send our children to school, so they could study hard, and not work and not grow up in a mill like us.

I told James about the cart and the roll of cloth and about Grace's father. He said he wanted to come and see for himself, so we agreed to meet that night, down by the canal.

There were no stars that night. I walked over the railway bridge. It had begun to snow heavily. I got to our meeting place but James wasn't there yet. The snow was falling thick and fast. "I hope he comes soon," I thought.

I waited fifteen minutes, but James didn't come.

I decided to go by myself. I didn't want to miss[6] the men. I walked quickly along the canal, leaving my footprints[7] in the fresh snow. When I came to the field, the men were already by the cart.

I hid behind the bushes and then a terrible thing happened. I tried to stop it but I couldn't. I waited until I could hardly breathe[8] and then I coughed.

The cough carried[9] across the white field to the cart. The men turned their heads towards me. They knew that someone was watching them. Then the red-haired man was running towards me. I knew his name now. It was Tom.

I knew I should run but I couldn't. I was frozen[10], frozen with cold or frozen with fear[11].

Then the coughing continued. Tom was standing by me. He had six children. Janet, the eldest, worked with me.

1 sore [sor] (a.) 疼痛發炎的
2 cottage [ˈkɑtɪdʒ] (n.) 農舍
3 grow [gro] (v.) 種植（動詞三態：grow; grew; grown）
4 keep [kip] (v.) 飼養（動詞三態：keep; kept; kept）
5 spin [spɪn] (v.) 紡織（動詞三態：spin; spun; spun）
6 miss [mɪs] (v.) 錯過
7 footprint [ˈfʊt͵prɪnt] (n.) 腳印
8 breathe [brið] (v.) 呼吸
9 carry [ˈkærɪ] (v.) 傳送
10 frozen [ˈfrozn̩] (a.) 凍住的
11 fear [fɪr] (n.) 害怕

"What are you doing here?" he asked. There was panic in his voice.

"You're stealing," I said.

Grace's father was here now. "Emily," he said in a shocked voice. "What are you doing here?"

"What do we do now?" asked Tom. "We can't let her go back home. She'll tell everyone. We'll lose our jobs and our homes."

"Does Grace know about this?" asked Grace's father.

I thought for a moment[1], then said quietly, "Yes."

Grace's father's face turned pale[2], pale as the snow falling around us. I felt sorry for him.

"She knows about the stealing, but she doesn't know it's you."

"Thank God," said Grace's father. "Does anybody else know?"

I decided to lie: "No," I said. "Just me and Grace. We went for a walk by the canal last week. We saw the barge stop and the men get off with the roll of cloth. We thought it was a dead body so we followed them to this cart."

"She can't go home," said Tom again. "We'll tie her up and leave her on the barge for the night. We need to plan what to do."

"OK," said Grace's father.

I looked into his eyes and I knew he could never hurt me, but I wasn't sure about Tom.

---

1 for a moment 片刻
2 pale [pel] (a.) 蒼白的

Quietly, I walked back to the canal with the two men. There was no point in trying to run away. My lungs were really bad that day and I was too weak[1].

It was still snowing and the canal was freezing over. They took me to a barge. Soon after we got to the barge, Grace's father left and went home. The other man, Tom, stayed to watch over me. I thought then that I was going to die.

Emily and Caterina

- Emily and Caterina are both in trouble. How are their situations similar? How are they different? Discuss in pairs.

I later learnt that James ran round to my house and banged loudly on the door. My father opened the door.

"Is Emily here?" James gasped[2], out of breath[3].

"No, she isn't. She's at Grace's house," said my father.

"Thanks," said James and he ran off down the path[4]. He knew I wasn't at Grace's house. He had just been there. He also knew that Grace's father wasn't there either. He knew I was in trouble[5]. He had to go and find me.

He ran over the railway bridge and down to the canal and then he saw something in the snow that looked like footprints. They were too small to be a man's.

1 weak [wik] (a.) 虛弱的
2 gasp [gæsp] (v.) 上氣不接下氣
3 out of breath 喘不過氣來
4 path [pæθ] (n.) 小徑
5 in trouble 惹上麻煩
6 struggle [ˈstrʌgl̩] (n.) 掙扎
7 frightened [ˈfraɪtn̩d] (a.) 害怕的
8 drop [drɑp] (v.) 丟下
9 evidence [ˈɛvədəns] (n.) 證據
10 branch [bræntʃ] (n.) 樹枝

"They could be Emily's," thought James, and he decided to follow them.

At first it was easy but the falling snow was covering everything fast. He followed them to the field and then there were lots of footprints, big and small.

"There's been a struggle[6]" thought James, and he was really frightened[7] now.

He went over to the old cart and he saw the roll of cloth on the ground. "Someone dropped[8] this, and they left in a hurry," he thought. "Emily was right. Someone is stealing cloth from the mill." This was all the evidence[9] he needed.

James looked around and then he followed what he thought were three sets of footprints back down to the canal. The branches[10] on the trees above the towpath[11] were by now heavy with snow.

James ran as fast as he could through the silence and the snow. The only sound was his heart beating[12] and his breath catching in his lungs.

Then suddenly he heard voices. He ran up the steep[13] path by the five locks[14] as best he could and then he saw me. I was wearing a blood red coat. My long black hair hung loose[15] around my shoulders.

The man pushed me and I screamed. The thin ice broke as I hit it and I was sucked[16] into its icy[17] depths[18].

---

11 towpath ['topæθ] (n.)
   （河道沿岸的）曳船路
12 heart beating 心跳
13 steep [stip] (a.) 陡峭的
14 lock [lɑk] (n.) 水閘
15 loose [lus] (a.) 鬆開的
16 suck [sʌk] (v.) 吞沒
17 icy ['aɪsɪ] (a.) 冰冷的
18 depth [dεpθ] (n.) 最深處

"No," screamed James, and he ran on up the path, slipping and sliding¹ in the snow. When James reached² the barge, he jumped into the canal but he knew he was too late. Nobody could survive this icy water.

As I sank deeper and deeper into the icy water, all my dreams sank with me. Yes, my dreams, for I had dreams, too. You know. I told you about them. But there's one more I haven't told you about. I was going to have a child and my child wasn't going to work in a mill. No, he was going to go to school and he was going to be a politician. He was going to save children like me.

But now that wasn't going to happen. Down and down I went. Down into the icy blackness and down my dreams went too.

Guess

- Do you think James will be able to save Emily?
- Do you think Emily's dreams will sink with her in the canal? Talk with a partner then share the class.

---

1 slip and slide 跌跌撞撞地滑行
2 reach [ritʃ] (v.) 到達

10. The barge

 When Caterina finally woke up, she felt cold and damp[1]. There was a terrible pain[2] in her head and a distinctive[3] sound – the *put put put* of a canal barge. She was on the canal, but why? The last thing she remembered was going to see Jake. "What happened after that? Think, girl; think!"

Then she remembered and her heart started beating fast.

"The shop – Uncle Sanjit – the two men. Where are they taking me?" Then her imagination[4] took over[5]. "They're going to throw me in the canal. It's all happening again. History is repeating itself. They're going to push me into the canal just like that man pushed my great-great grandmother," thought Caterina. "Perhaps this is the canal at Saltaire or is that too much of a coincidence[6]? Samira wouldn't think so. Samira would say it's my destiny[7]."

Suddenly there was a very loud sound of fast moving water. "Oh, no! The barge is sinking."

Caterina screamed but her scream could not compete[8] with the sound of water. Water poured down on them, but the barge didn't sink, and then it clicked[9]. "Now, I know what's happening," Caterina thought. "It's OK. We're in a lock," she thought and she breathed a sigh of relief. Then she had an idea. "I'll count the locks. Then I'll know where we are."

1 damp [dæmp] (a.) 潮濕的
2 pain [pen] (n.) 痛
3 distinctive [dɪˈstɪŋktɪv] (a.) 特殊的
4 imagination [ɪˌmædʒəˈneʃən] (n.) 想像力
5 take over 接管
6 coincidence [koˈɪnsɪdəns] (n.) 巧合
7 destiny [ˈdɛstənɪ] (n.) 命運
8 compete [kəmˈpit] (v.) 競爭
9 click [klɪk] (v.) 發出卡嗒聲

And so Caterina counted. "Five locks! There's only one place in the whole country with five locks. I know where we are."

Put put put, the engine stopped and the barge came to a halt[1]. She heard the men tie up the barge – then footsteps as they walked away.

"Are they coming back? How much time do I have to escape[2]?" she wondered.

There was a chain around her left leg and it was locked to the door. She couldn't escape. Her hands were free but there was nothing she could do.

Then, Caterina felt her phone in her pocket.

"If only I can text[3] Jake. I can tell him where I am. He'll know what to do." Quickly, she pulled the phone out of her pocket and went to messages.

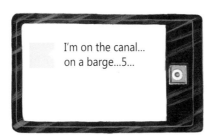

I'm on the canal...
on a barge...5...

Just then Caterina heard a voice and fear overcame[4] her. The barge rocked[5] as someone climbed on. Caterina panicked[6]. "I have to send it now," she thought. Her hands trembled[7] as she hit the send button. Hopefully Jake would understand where she was. She lay down on the floor again and shut her eyes. Now she could hear voices at the other end of the barge.

1 halt [hɔlt] (n.) 停止
2 escape [ə`skep] (v.) 逃脫
3 text [tɛkst] (v.) 發簡訊
4 overcome [,ovə`kʌm] (v.)
　戰勝 (動態三態：overcome;
　overcame; overcome)
5 rock [rɑk] (v.) 搖晃
6 panic [`pænɪk] (v.) 恐慌 (動詞三態：
　panic; panicked; panicked)
7 tremble [`trɛmbl̩] (v.) 顫抖

"Are you going to check on the girl?" said a voice.

"No. She's not going anywhere – not with that chain around her foot! Anyway, she's still unconscious[1]. She hit her head really hard. What are we going to do with her anyway?"

"I don't know yet," said Sid. "We could sink the barge with her in it."

"You're joking[2], right?" said Aamir, shocked.

"Maybe, maybe not!" said Sid smiling. "But one thing's for sure, she's not going anywhere until Sanjit pays us for the material. And then, when we've got the money, we disappear back to London."

"And leave her to a cold and watery death," finished Aamir, scared.

"Who said anything about death? You watch too many horror[3] films[4]," said Sid, slapping Aamir on the back.

"Please, Jake. Please, Jake. Please understand the message," Caterina whispered over and over again to herself as she lay in the darkness.

No message from Caterina. Ten minutes later, still no message.

Jake doodled[5] on his notepad. Half an hour, still no message.

More doodling. "Maybe she just doesn't want to answer my message."

More doodling. "But what if something has happened? What could happen in the time it takes to walk from my house to Caterina's house?"

---

1 unconscious [ʌnˈkɑnʃəs] (a.) 不省人事的
2 joke [dʒok] (v.) 開玩笑
3 horror [ˈhɔrɚ] (n.) 恐怖
4 film [fɪlm] (n.) 電影
5 doodle [ˈdudl̩] (v.) 塗鴉

Jake paced⁶ the room now. "What if she didn't go home? What if she followed my uncle?"

An hour later... Two hours later...

Ting Ting Caterina's name flashed up on Jake's mobile and there was the message:

"I'm on the canal...on a barge...5..."

5 what? What can she mean? I've never been on the canal. I don't know what she means. Does she mean 5 bridges, 5 towns, 5 what? Jake needed help. Quickly he texted his best friend Simon:

"Meet me at the canal at Saltaire ASAP⁷. Caterina's in trouble."

Simon didn't know Caterina. Jake deleted⁸ her name and put:

"I'm in trouble. Read this: I'm on the canal...on a barge...5... Does the 5 mean anything to you? Tell me when we meet up."

Ting Ting "I'm on my way. 5? I'll have a think."

The message smiled at him. Jake grabbed his coat and put the diary into his pocket. He didn't know why he was taking it. Maybe there was something in it that would help them find Caterina.

Once outside, he unchained⁹ his bike and got on it. It wasn't snowing any more, but the snow still lay¹⁰ thick on the ground.

Jake pedaled¹¹ as fast as he could through the silent white world. The number five went round and round his head.

When Jake got to Saltaire, Simon was standing on the railway bridge waiting for him.

---

6 pace [pes] (v.) 踱步
7 ASAP (adv.) 盡快地 (as soon as possible 的字首縮寫)
8 delete [dɪˈlit] (v.) 刪除
9 unchain [ʌnˈtʃen] (v.) 解開鎖鏈
10 lie [laɪ] (v.) 置於；躺 (動詞三態：lie; lay; lain)
11 pedal [ˈpɛdl̩] (v.) 踩踏板

1 brake [brek] (v.) 煞車
2 skid [skɪd] (v.) 打滑
3 slope [slop] (n.) 斜坡
4 spray [spre] (v.) 濺散
5 What took you? 你怎麼這麼久？
6 gear [gɪr] (n.) 齒輪
7 grip [grɪp] (v.) 緊握
8 stare [stɛr] (v.) 盯；凝視
9 get it 懂

"Five"– the mill was on the canal. Maybe Caterina meant five mill windows or five mill chimneys. Were there five mill chimneys? Jake didn't know.

He braked[1] hard and his bike skidded[2] down the slope[3], spraying[4] snow everywhere until finally it came to a halt just in front of Simon.

"Impressive! What took you?[5]"

"We don't all have expensive bikes with twenty gear[6] and special snow tires," said Jake.

"Yeah, right. I wish."

"So have you worked out what 'five' means?" asked Jake.

"Maybe. Have you?" asked Simon.

"No, but I think it's something to do with the mill. It's just a feeling," said Jake, pushing his hands in his pockets and gripping[7] the small leather book with his icy cold fingers.

"Well, I don't," said Simon. "There's only one five on the canal and that's the Five-rise Locks."

"Of course. That's where Caterina is," said Jake.

"Caterina? Who's Caterina? And what's she got to do with all this?"

"Caterina?" said Jake. "Umh... Caterina's the girl who's organizing the protest outside my uncle's shop on Saturday."

"Oh, yeah. I remember," said Simon. "The girl who you ran off to see during basketball practice this afternoon."

"Yes, her," said Jake staring[8] at the ground and kicking at the snow with his right foot.

"I still don't get it[9]," said Simon.

"She's in trouble, not me. Now come on. She really is in trouble."

Simon was about to tease[1] his friend but then he saw the scared look in his eyes.

"How far away are the five locks?" asked Jake.

"About ten or fifteen minutes if we pedal fast," said Simon getting onto his bike. "Come on. I'll race you there."

It was hard pedaling along the snowy towpath, but Jake was determined. He soon sped[2] far ahead of Simon.

When he got to the five locks, he got off his bike and left it at the bottom of the steep slope. Up he ran, slipping and sliding in the snow. He could see an old barge tied at the top. Jake ran the last few meters as fast as he could. He was almost opposite the barge now.

He looked over at it and saw Caterina's face pressed up against one of the windows. She saw him, too.

"There's nobody here," she called. "They've left me here."

Jake saw the terror in her eyes and he saw her mouth opening and closing, but he couldn't hear her properly[3].

He ran over the bridge to the other side of the canal and jumped onto the barge. Splash[4]! Jake looked down in horror at the water around his feet.

"The barge is sinking," he thought. Quickly, he found the room where Caterina was.

"It's sinking; we haven't got much time," he said.

"I know," said Caterina. "They've left the key to the padlock in the kitchen. They told me. They didn't want to kill me. They just didn't want me to speak to your uncle."

"Who?" asked Jake. "Who did this?"

"Jake, we don't have time to talk now. I'll explain everything later. Go and find the key to this padlock and let's get off this barge before it sinks."

"But they put a hole in the barge. They wanted you to die," said Jake. "They're murderers[5]."

"I don't think they put a hole in the barge. It just happened. It's old," said Caterina. "Now go and get the key."

Jake went to the kitchen. The key was by the sink. It was easy to find. "Maybe Caterina's right. Maybe they didn't want her to die," thought Jake.

---

1 tease [tiz] (v.) 取笑
2 speed [spid] (v.) 迅速前進（動詞三態：speed; sped, speeded; sped, speeded）
3 properly [ˈprɑpəlɪ] (adv.)〔口〕完全地
4 splash [splæʃ] (v.) 潑濕；濺起
5 murderer [ˈmɝdərə] (n.) 兇手

Quickly, Jake took the key and went back to unlock the padlock. The lock was old. Jake tried to unlock it but he couldn't. He looked down at the water. It was above his ankles now.

"The water's rising fast," he thought, "We've got to get out of here soon."

Simon was here now. "Are you alright, Jake? Do you want some help down there?"

"No. Don't get on the barge. You'll only make it sink faster," Jake shouted back anxiously[1]. "Call an ambulance."

Jake's fingers were stiff[2] and cold. He couldn't stop them from trembling. He was scared, but he didn't want Caterina to know that.

"What if I can't unlock the padlock?" he thought. "I can't leave Caterina on the barge by herself. I'll have to stay with her. We'll die together. Yeah, right. That's so not going to happen. Of course we'll get off the barge. This isn't the Titanic, is it? And this isn't an ocean. It's the Leeds-Liverpool canal."

He turned the key one more time and the padlock came open.

"I've done it," he said and he gave Caterina a hug[3]. Then they both stared at each other embarrassed.

"Thanks," she said quietly. "I thought that was the end."

Suddenly the front of the barge sank forward[4].

"Come on. Let's get off before it's too late," shouted Jake.

Simon was there on the towpath looking worried. He helped them climb off. Then they all stood and watched the barge sink as they waited for the ambulance.

---

1 anxiously [ˈæŋkʃəslɪ] (adv.) 緊張不安地
2 stiff [stɪf] (a.) 僵硬的
3 hug [hʌg] (n.) 緊抱
4 forward [ˈfɔrwəd] (adv.) 向前

5 siren [ˈsaɪrən] (n.) 警報器
6 flash [flæʃ] (v.) 閃亮
7 paramedic [ˌpærəˈmɛdɪk] (n.) 醫護人員

Jake pushed his hands in his pockets. There was nothing there.

"The diary – I've lost the diary," thought Jake. "It was in my coat pocket but it's not there any more. Now I'll never know what happened to Emily. And how am I going to tell Caterina? She loves that diary."

The ambulance finally arrived, sirens[5] screaming and lights flashing[6]. The paramedics[7] ran over to them and Jake forgot about the diary.

11. Emily's Dream

It was a sunny Saturday morning. Caterina and her friends walked purposefully[1] along the street to Boho Chic. They were all excited and a little nervous. They each had a handful of leaflets.

"So, we're really going to do this," said Samira.

"Of course," said Caterina. "I've put too much work into it. I'm not going to back out[2] now. You're not nervous, are you?"

"A bit," said Samira. "I've never done anything like this before."

"It'll be alright," said Caterina and linked[3] arms with Samira.

They chatted happily as they walked along.

"Tell us again what happened that night," begged Samira.

"And you say Jake rescued[4] you. Wow! Lucky you!" said Helena.

Jake and Uncle Sanjit were standing on the steps of Boho Chic waiting for them. They'd taken down the brown paper from the shop windows and everyone could see the window displays.

"Wow! The shop looks amazing[5]," said Caterina.

"Thanks for coming along," said Uncle Sanjit. "And for writing the leaflets."

"Jake helped me," said Caterina. "He did all the illustrations[6]."

"I know. He's good, isn't he?" Then he turned to face the others. "Right. Everyone to their places now," he said. "And no chatting. You're here to work. You can all talk in the café later."

"Yes, readers, you've guessed. I've called the protest off. We're not here to hand out protest leaflets. We're here to hand out promotion[7] leaflets for Boho Chic. But you still don't know the ending to Emily's story, do you? I'll tell you later. First let me bring you up-to-date[8] on Boho Chic. Uncle Sanjit found some new suppliers who really do buy their cotton from a small farm in India. And guess what? He's promised to take me to visit the cotton farm in the summer holidays. Sid and Aamir's court case[9] is next month. I'm really nervous about that. I don't want to think about it now. Of course, the shop opening today is a huge success. Uncle Sanjit's designs are amazing. Well, so all my friends say, and I agree."

1 purposefully [ˈpɝpəsfʊlɪ] (adv.) 有目的地
2 back out 取消
3 link [lɪŋk] (v.) 勾住（手臂）
4 rescue [ˈrɛskju] (v.) 搭救
5 amazing [əˈmezɪŋ] (a.) 驚人的
6 illustration [ɪˌlʌsˈtreʃən] (n.) 插圖
7 promotion [prəˈmoʃən] (n.) 促銷
8 up-to-date [ˈʌptəˈdet] (a.) 最新訊息的
9 court case 審判案

After the shop closed, Caterina and Jake had a drink in the shop café. They were waiting for Uncle Sanjit and the staff[1] to finish cashing up[2].

"Caterina, there's something I have to tell you," said Jake.

Caterina looked up from her drink. Jake looked serious.

"What?" asked Caterina, worried.

"That night when I rescued you from the canal barge, I had the diary with me and..." he paused and looked at Caterina.

"And?" said Caterina.

"And I lost it," said Jake miserably[3].

"Is that all?" asked Caterina, relieved.

"You mean you're not mad at me?"

"No. I typed[4] the whole diary up on my laptop. So it's not lost."

"Then can you tell me the end of the story? I didn't finish it and I really want to know what happened to Emily. Did she die?"

"She can't have died, can she? If she'd died, I wouldn't be here, would I, silly?" said Caterina and she laughed. Then she looked serious. "Emily didn't die, but she didn't get her fairy-tale[5] ending."

"Did she marry James?"

"Yes, she did but they never moved away to the Lake District. They stayed in Saltaire. She did have a son, but he didn't go to university and he didn't become a politician. He worked in the mill."

"So you must make her dream come true[6]."

"Yeah, very funny. I wish," said Caterina.

1 staff [stæf] (n.) 工作人員
2 cash up 數錢
3 miserably [ˋmɪzərəblɪ] (adv.) 可憐兮兮地
4 type [taɪp] (v.) 打字
5 fairy-tale [ˋfɛrɪ͵tel] (a.) 童話故事般的
6 dream come true 美夢成真

Ⓐ Personal Response

1. Did you like the story? Why/why not?

2. Could this story take place in your country? If not, why not?

3. Which part of the story did you enjoy most? Explain why.

4. What did you think of Caterina's ideas and actions? Would you do the same in her situation?

5. Is there anything you would like to change in the story? Give details.

6. What are the important messages in the story? Do you agree with them?

7. Did you like the ending of the story? Did you find it surprising? What did you think would happen?

8. Suggest other ways in which the story could end.

9. Have you ever read a story like this before?

10. Do you think this story would make a good film? Why/why not?

❸ Comprehension

Emily's story

1 Tick (✓) true (T) or false (F).

T F ⓐ Charles Dickens published *A Tale of Two Cities* in 1859.

T F ⓑ Emily was Caterina's grandmother.

T F ⓒ Emily and her friends worked in a clothes shop.

T F ⓓ Grace's father was stealing cloth from the mill.

T F ⓔ Emily was afraid of Grace's father.

T F ⓕ Tom pushed Emily into the icy cold canal.

T F ⓖ Emily drowned in the canal.

2 Correct the false sentences and write true sentences.

3 How many of these small details in the story did you notice? Complete the sentences.

ⓐ In 1853, Emily's parents found work at the new .... mill outside Bradford.

ⓑ Emily's family had a bigger house than the others because her father was an ....

ⓒ Because of the dust Emily and her friends had difficulty ....

ⓓ Emily thought there was a .... in the package that the two men hid under the cart.

ⓔ Grace's father had no money, but he always bought his children ....

ⓕ James searched for Emily everywhere. Finally he saw some .... in the snow and he followed them.

ⓖ James ran up the steep path by the .... Then he saw Emily.

Caterina's story

4 Number the events in the order they happened.

_____ a) Jake asked Caterina to call off the protest, but she refused.

_____ b) Caterina overheard the suppliers saying that they had lied to Uncle Sanjit: the cotton was picked in Uzbekistan.

_____ c) Caterina found a little leather book with the story of Emily's life.

_____ d) The suppliers kidnapped Caterina and left her on an old barge on the canal.

_____ e) Caterina decided to protest about child labor outside Uncle Sanjit's new shop.

_____ f) Caterina followed Uncle Sanjit to a meeting with his suppliers.

_____ g) Jake learnt that Emily didn't drown in the canal and that she married James.

_____ h) Everybody went to the opening of Uncle Sanjit's shop. It was a big success.

_____ i) Jake rescued Caterina from the sinking barge.

_____ j) Caterina fell and banged her head becoming unconscious.

5 Answer the questions with the name of a character from the story.

a) Whose grandfather came from India to work in the mills in England?

b) Who wants to go to the London School of Economics?

c) Who went to St Martins College to study fashion?

d) Who lied to Uncle Sanjit?

e) Whose uncle owned the old barge where they kept Caterina?

f) Who knows that the number five means the five locks?

g) Who found the key to unlock the padlock and rescued Caterina?

C Characters

1 Which characteristics do Emily and Caterina share?
Tick the adjectives.

- ○ determined
- ○ cautious
- ○ brave
- ○ cruel
- ○ ambitious
- ○ kind

- ○ greedy
- ○ sensible
- ○ caring
- ○ selfish
- ○ impulsive

2 Work with a partner. Take it in turns to choose a character,
and describe him/her to your partner using the adjectives
below or any others you can think of. Your partner has to
guess which character you are talking about.

Sid   Uncle Sanjit   Jake   Grace

ambitious   artistic   creative   dishonest
sad   sporty   superstitious   unethical
unlucky   violent

3 In pairs, discuss the characters' motives.

a. Grace's father was a good man. He loved his children. Why did he steal the cloth?

b. Why didn't Emily run away from the two men?

c. Why did Tom push Emily into the canal?

d. Caterina was organizing a protest outside Uncle Sanjit's new shop. Why was she organizing it? Why did Sanjit want to stop it?

e. Why did Sid and Aamir kidnap Caterina?

f. Jake asked Simon to meet him at the canal as soon as possible. Why?

4 Complete the paragraph about Emily with the words below.

eight years old   school   mill
children like her   easy   1851
great-great grandmother   Lake District

Emily was Caterina's (a) .... She was born in (b) .... in Bradford, and she didn't have an

(c) .... life. She didn't go to

(d) .... Instead, she started working in a mill when she was (e) .... She hated working in the mill and she wanted to go and live in a small cottage in the (f) .... If she had a son, she wanted him to be a politician and save (g) .... She got married and she had a son, but he didn't become a politician. He worked in a (h) .... , too.

5 Match the sentences to the characters.

Jake

James

Simon

Sid

_____ a His father was an overlooker.

_____ b He guessed where Caterina was.

_____ c All the girls thought he was very good-looking.

_____ d He was Jake's best friend.

_____ e He loved Emily.

_____ f Caterina was frightened of him.

_____ g He supplied the cotton to Uncle Sanjit.

_____ h He wanted to study art.

6 Choose one of the characters from Exercise 5. Write a paragraph about him.

D Plot and Theme

1 One of the main themes of the story is child labor. How much do you know about child labor? Do the quiz and find out. Then listen to check your answers.

a Worldwide, ... million children work.
1 12   2 250   3 20   4 125

b One in .... 5-14 year old children work in developing countries.
1 two   2 ten   3 six   4 five

c School is important. Children of educated mothers are .... more likely to live beyond age 5.
1 40%   2 60%   3 20%   4 30%

d .... million 15-24 year olds will not be able to read or write in 2015.
1 25   2 50   3 10   4 105

e At the time of the 2002 World Cup, around .... children in Pakistan were employed making footballs for less than 70 cents a day.
1 1,000   2 15,000   3 5,000   4 10,000

2 Go back to Caterina's leaflet on pages 22 and 23. In groups of three, discuss other types of child labor. Can you think of or find out about any charities or organizations which help to work against child labor. Present your research to the class.

3 Which events happen in both stories? Read and tick.

———— [a] There is a kidnapping.

———— [b] A canal barge sinks.

———— [c] Two men steal cloth from the mill.

———— [d] A girl is rescued from the canal.

———— [e] It snows.

———— [f] Somebody tells a lie.

4 Put these events from Caterina and Emily's stories in the correct order.

———— [a] Caterina met Uncle Sanjit.

———— [b] Caterina planned to protest at the opening of Uncle Sanjit's new shop.

———— [c] Caterina and Jake wrote and designed a leaflet for the opening of Boho Chic.

———— [d] Jake rescued Caterina from a sinking barge.

———— [e] Caterina was kidnapped by Aamir and Sid.

———— [a] The two men kidnapped Emily and pushed her into the canal.

———— [b] Emily and her friend Grace discovered some men stealing cloth from the mill.

———— [c] Emily's parents started working at Salts Mill.

———— [d] Emily's boyfriend James dived into the canal to rescue her.

———— [e] Emily discovered one of the men was Grace's father.

E Language

1 Which adjectives are used to describe the nouns below?
Match and write.

icy   trendy   cheap   flared   polluted   chesty

a _____ scarves   d _____ trousers
b _____ cough   e _____ river
c _____ clothes   f _____ water

2 Complete the sentences with the noun and adjective pairs
from the exercise above.

a People wore .... in the 1970s.
b The red-haired man had a terrible ....
c No fish lived in the ....
d She convinced him not to buy any more ....
e Simon was very fashionable. He always wore ....
f Nobody could swim in the .... It was too cold.

3 Match the everyday expressions from the story with their
meanings.

a Jump to it.   1 I don't understand.
b It's just a feeling.   2 It's important to you.
c You're joking, right?   3 I felt very sad.
d I don't get it.   4 You used to live in this area.
e I know it means a lot to you.   5 I don't want to ...
f My heart sank.   6 You're not telling the truth,
g It costs next to nothing.   are you?
h Don't jump to conclusions.   7 Find out all the facts before
i I don't fancy ...   you decide something.
j You're from round here.   8 It's just an idea.
                                   9 Do it now.
                                  10 It's very cheap.

4 Complete the sentences with the past simple or the past passive of the verbs below.

be   carry   write   open
record   publish   invent   start

a   *A Tale of Two Cities* .... in 1859.
b   Big Ben .... ticking in 1859.
c   The Suez Canal .... in 1869.
d   Leo Tolstoy .... *War and Peace* in 1869.
e   The vacuum cleaner .... in 1869.
f   Skylab 3 .... the first fish into space in the 1970s.
g   "I Will Survive"................ in the 1970s.
h   The film, *Grease* .... a box office hit in the 1970s.

5 Find out about and then write sentences about the items below.

Wuthering Heights   the iPhone   the laptop
Pride and Prejudice   the television

a _____
b _____
c _____
d _____
e _____

6 Choose a decade and write five sentences about it in your notebook.

TEST

 1 Read the story again and tick (✓) true (T) or false (F).

T **F** ⓐ Dust from the mills gave lots of workers bad coughs.

T **F** ⓑ The mills were quiet and safe places to work.

T **F** ⓒ Jake and Caterina visited Salts Mill on a school trip.

T **F** ⓓ Caterina was happy that her friends could buy trendy clothes cheaply.

T **F** ⓔ Uncle Sanjit wasn't concerned about where his cotton came from.

T **F** ⓕ Caterina went home after talking to Jake and Sanjit.

T **F** ⓖ Emily and her friends often went shopping at Brown & Muff.

T **F** ⓗ Grace found out her father was stealing cloth from the mill.

T **F** ⓘ Emily was discovered because of her cough and Caterina because of her phone.

T **F** ⓙ Emily managed to persuade Grace's father to take her home.

T **F** ⓚ Caterina didn't understand where she was on the barge.

T **F** ⓛ Jake understood Caterina's text message straight away.

T **F** ⓜ James found Emily because of the tracks in the snow.

T **F** ⓝ Neither James nor Jake managed to save Emily or Caterina.

T **F** ⓞ Caterina decided not to protest against Uncle Sanjit's new shop.

2 Correct the false sentences.

P **3** Read and choose the correct answers.

a Emily is .... years old when she starts work at the mill.

  ① six   ② eight   ③ twelve   ④ sixteen

b The .... was invented in 1869.

  ① TV   ② telephone   ③ escalator   ④ vacuum cleaner

c In Bradford, ... percent of mill workers' children were dead by the age of fifteen.

  ① ten   ② fifteen   ③ twenty   ④ thirty

d Jake finds Caterina because she ....

  ① sends him a text message
  ② phones him
  ③ shouts and he hears her
  ④ leaves him a note

e James finds Emily because ....

  ① Grace's father tells him where she is
  ② she sends him a text message
  ③ Grace helps him
  ④ he sees her footprints in the snow

f In the end, Emily ....

  ① moves to the Lake District
  ② marries James and continues working in the mill
  ③ drowns in the canal
  ④ becomes a politician

P **4** In pairs, choose two different pictures in the book. Take turns telling each other what you can see in your picture.

 01 Find out about Fairtrade.

What is Fairtrade? Fairtrade makes sure that:

- farmers earn enough money to support their families and have a better future.
- farmers and workers have safe and healthy working conditions through fairer trading conditions, fair prices and a premium (extra money).
- child labor is not permitted and immediate action is always taken to stop this when it happens.

The natural environment is protected by:

- reducing the amount of chemicals used
- saving water
- producing less waste

Listen to the story of a group of Fairtrade cocoa farmers. Write a short text about them including the words below.

West Africa
chocolate bar
afford
earn
Divine
shares
charity
Comic Relief
wrapper
competition

作者簡介

Elspeth，你好，跟我們介紹一下你自己吧。

我大學是讀戲劇的，曾在倫敦一家戲劇報社工作過，後來決定去接受師資訓練，擔任英語教師。在命運奇妙的安排下，我在土耳其的伊斯坦堡謀得一份教職，從此就一直居住在伊斯坦堡，從事教書和寫作的工作。

你的故事靈感是怎麼來的？

我故事的靈感大都來自於旅行地點，我感覺到我會喜歡讀場景設在當地的故事。

你為什麼選擇薩爾茨紡織廠來當做這篇故事的場景？

有些地方會讓人印象特別深刻，薩爾茨紡織廠就是這樣一個地方。那裡以前是一家大型的舊式紡織廠，不過現在已經搖身一變成為美術館了。紡織廠的歷史和紡織廠老闆的事蹟都很引人入勝，那裡是設定一篇神祕故事場景的絕佳地點。

這篇故事的主題是什麼？

這篇故事的主題在講工時超長、工作環境惡劣的童工。故事中的角色虛構的，但是在過去，的確有很多像愛蜜麗和葛麗絲這樣的年輕女孩在薩爾茨紡織廠工作，而且也有很多女孩年紀輕輕就因此過世。在今天的世界裡，還是有童工在惡劣的環境中工作，而且年紀輕輕就去世。

我想特別感謝羅傑‧克拉克，他是一位作家和當地的歷史學家，他協助我研究紡織廠的歷史背景。而我第一次拜訪紡織廠，是我媽媽帶我去的。

1. 日記

P.13

　　時值 1859 年，這一年，查爾斯·達爾文的《物種起源》問世，倫敦國會的大笨鐘滴滴答答地開始運轉，英國文豪查爾斯·狄更斯出版了《雙城記》。當此之際，工業革命已經改變了英國的面貌，我的曾曾祖母也開始在布拉福的薩爾茨羊毛紡織廠工作，那一年她正值十八年華。

　　空氣中都是白色的細毛絮，簡直快嗆死我啦；機器的聲音震耳欲聾，手都不知道到底是要遮眼睛還是摀耳朵。我想轉身逃出去，可是有一雙大手把我推回房裡。我想放聲大叫，但沒有人會聽得到。
　　我一輩子都忘不了第一天去薩爾茨紡織廠上工的情況。

　　愛蜜麗

　　今年是 2012 年，卡特瑞娜正坐在學校餐廳角落裡的一個餐桌上。現在是午餐時間，她可以聽到嘈雜的人聲和碗盤刀叉的鏗鏘聲。

P.14

　　傑可吃完午餐準備離開餐廳時，看到了卡特瑞娜。她的一頭紅色長髮往後紮成馬尾，他這時看不到她的眼睛，但他知道她有一雙綠色的眸子。她正在讀著什麼的，大概是在看那張鬧得滿城風雨的傳單吧。他得找她談一下這件事情，

現在正是時候吧。
　　卡特瑞娜正重覆讀著傳單的第一段，一個身影從桌子對面投射下來，接著她聽到對面的椅子往後拉的聲音。她抬起頭，看到了傑可。傑可的個頭很高，有一頭深棕色頭髮和一雙深棕色的眼睛，人們大都會說他長得很帥，有一張迷死人的笑容，不過他這時並沒有擺出笑臉。
　　「卡特瑞娜，你要做的這件事情並不公平。」他說，「那是我桑吉特叔叔的店，他可是拚命工作攢了好幾年的錢，才開了這家店的。」他補充道。
　　「那他對店裡所賣的東西就應該更謹慎才對啊，做那些衣服的人，都是比我們還小的小朋友耶。」卡特瑞娜閃爍著綠色的眸子，反駁地說道。
　　「因為我們上個月去參觀過薩爾茨紡織廠，所以你才看不過去，對不對？」他說，「這也沒什麼不對，我們大家都看不過去。」他繼續說道。

•你最近有什麼看不過去的事嗎？

P.15

「才不是呢⋯⋯好吧，你要這樣說也可以啦。工廠和童工早就應該絕跡，但他們實際上還存在，對不對？你戴的圍巾是誰做的？你花了多少錢買到的？」

「五英鎊。」傑可驕傲地回答道。

「你有沒有問過你自己，怎麼會賣得這麼便宜？」

「沒。你要說的是什麼？」

「我要說的是，就是因為在世界的另一邊有一些兒童過著悲慘的生活，才讓你有這些時尚的衣服可以穿！」卡特瑞娜忿忿不平地說。

「我不管這個圍巾是誰做的，我只是要跟你說，你不可以在我叔叔的店門口發傳單！」傑可說。

「來不及啦，傳單都印好了。」卡特瑞娜說。

「這又不是亞洲的血汗工廠，這是布拉福。況且它講的這也不是現在的布拉福，而是兩百年前左右的布拉福！」傑可訝異地說。

「第一頁講的是歷史，其他頁講的是當今兒童的生活。」卡特瑞娜說。

「那這是什麼？」傑可指著第一段說：「這看起來像是從日記或信件裡摘錄下來的段落。」

卡特瑞娜說：「不完全是，愛蜜麗不識字，不會寫字，沒受過教育。」她從袋子裡拿出一本皮質封面的本子，遞給傑可，「我奶奶上個星期去世了。」她補了一句說道。

P.16

「喔，我不知道這件事，我感到遺憾。」傑可喃喃地說道。

「她走了。這是我在她的閣樓裡找到的本子。」

「那誰是愛蜜麗？她不可能是妳奶奶，1859 年時，你奶奶還沒有出生。」傑可問。

「不是我奶奶，愛蜜麗是我的曾曾祖母。她跟我奶奶講她的事，然後我奶奶就幫她把故事寫在這個小本子上，我傳單上引用的內容就是從這裡出來的。如果你想看，可以借你看，很好看喔！」卡特瑞娜說。

「改天吧！」傑可一邊說，一邊闔上皮質封面的小本子，把本子推回去給桌子對面的卡特瑞娜，「我現在要去練籃球了。」

卡特瑞娜等著他起身，但他沒有起

身，反倒是盯著她的臉瞧。「所有的女生都在肖想他，但我可沒興趣，我還有更重要的事要思考。」她想。

傑可這時皺了一下眉頭，「這件事你是認真的，是嗎？」

「當然，我是很認真的。」卡特瑞娜答。

「我叔叔不會感謝你讓他的店關門大吉的。」

「是沒錯，但在亞洲的那些女生也不會太感恩每週工作七十個小時，賺取微薄的工錢，來供應你叔叔做那種不正派的生意。」卡特瑞娜回答說。

P.18

傑可仍睜大眼睛盯著她看，桌子上那本小本子還擱放在他們中間。卡特瑞娜可以感覺到旁人正一邊看著他們，一邊竊竊私語。根本沒什麼好看、好講的啊，她和傑可之間又不可能有什麼，永遠不可能。

傑可站了起來。

「再見啦。」他說完後便離開。卡特瑞娜看著他走過餐廳，消失在眼前。

她桌子旁的空間很快擠滿了好奇的女生，「傑可想幹嘛？」「他想約你出去嗎？」

「當然不是啊！」卡特瑞娜生氣地說，然後把皮質封面的本子塞回袋子裡。

她現在不想給其他任何人看這個本子，她也搞不清楚自己為什麼要拿給傑可看。「他當然不會有興趣啊，我真蠢，幹嘛拿給他看！」她心想。

「那他幹嘛找你？」女生們追問。

「你們那麼想知道啊，他啊，要我星期六不要去他叔叔的店門口抗議。」卡特瑞娜說。

「那你還是要去嗎？」海倫娜問。大家都知道她星期六要去抗議。

「當然啦，還是要去！」卡特瑞娜一邊說，一邊拿起她的包包，走出餐廳。

2. 超便宜的圍巾

P.19

傑可射籃，竟連籃框都沒有碰到。他在傳單上看到的愛蜜麗的那段話，揮之不去。他現在很想看那本皮質封面的小本子，想繼續往下讀愛蜜麗的故事，可是他又不能跟卡特瑞娜說，不是嗎？他以前壓根沒想過布拉福的歷史，也沒想過布拉福是如何演變成今天這個樣子的。歷史重演的過程是很奇特，某個時空的歷史，竟在另一個時空中重演，實在是很奇怪，難道人們是不記取歷史教訓的？

「嘿，傑可，你沒接到我的傳球！」賽門一邊說道，一邊拍拍傑可的背，把傑可的心思拉回到球場，「你怎麼啦？」

「沒事。」傑可說：「這個，很抱歉，我要先走。」

「你可別說是為了餐廳裡的那個女生喔，不會吧？你是被電到還是怎樣？」

「當然不是啊，我是有事要先走啦。」

「不能等打完球再走嗎？」

「沒辦法。」傑可說完便離開體育館。

P.20

他聽到隊友喊他留下來，但他未加以理會。隊友會發火，也是理所當然的，他能理解。他們星期天有一場重要的比賽要打，得加緊練習，只是他無法專心練球，多留無益。

他看看手錶，現在還是午餐時間。「卡特瑞娜現在可能還在餐廳吧。」他心想，然後立刻往餐廳跑去。

現在時間有點晚了，餐廳裡的學生不多，而卡特瑞娜仍坐在那裡讀著皮質封面的小本子。

「謝天謝地，你還在！」傑可一邊走向卡特瑞娜，一邊說道。

「傑可，你現在找我有什麼事？」卡特瑞娜說。

「我找你，是因為我在想你那個傳單的事情，我想看那本小本子。」傑可很快地說道。

「真的假的？」卡特瑞娜說。

「真的！我一直在想你跟我說的事，我想多知道一點。」他停了一下，「我爺爺一九五〇年代時從印度來到這裡，在一家工廠裡工作。我爺爺和你曾曾祖母的時代相隔很遠，但我知道情況並沒有怎麼改善。」

「沒錯，不過起碼你爺爺是成年人。你讀讀看這個，你讀完之後就不會想買那些超便宜的圍巾了！」卡特瑞娜說。

卡特瑞娜把小本子交給傑可。這一次，傑可坐下來讀了本子。

P.22

沒錯，這件 T 恤很炫，但是你知道以下這些問題的答案嗎？你知道 T 恤的棉花是從那裡採集來的嗎？更重要的是，是什麼人在採集棉花的？你在衣服的標籤上看不到這些問題的答案，對吧？那麼讓我來告訴你吧！

「童工」並不是過去才有的事情，從埃及到印度，從巴基斯坦到墨西哥，全世界各地有數百萬兒童，他們工作時數超長，幫你製作你所穿的衣服。

我叫亞吉，我住在烏茲別克，烏茲別克是全球主要的棉花出口國之一。每年秋天時，鎮上的學校就會關閉，所有的學生都會跟著老師去棉花田工作。約有一百萬名五歲至十四歲的兒童，會去棉花田打工。去年，我被送到一個離家很遠的棉花農場，待在沒有窗戶也沒有電的房間裡工作，一公斤的棉花可以掙到三或四分錢。這樣，這件 T 恤還很不錯嗎？

P.23

我叫雅妮卡，十二歲，住在孟加拉。我爸爸、媽媽都在成衣廠工作，因為收入不多，所以無法供應我去上學。我和我妹妹都要去工廠工作，而我妹妹才九歲大。當你出門去和朋友玩時，你頭上帶的帽兜，搞不好就是我做的。

那頂棒球帽看起來很不錯，你知道去年工作了多少小時在縫帽子嗎？我叫做帕瑞蜜塔，十二歲，住在印度的德里。我奶奶生病了，亟需醫藥費，所以就讓我去工作。我以前有上學校，不過現在每天工作十二小時。

P. 24

「好吧，你贏了，我不想再買便宜貨的圍巾了。不過，我還是希望你星期六不要去我叔叔的店門口站崗。」傑可說。接著他想到那本小本子，他很想讀看看，只是卡特瑞娜還會借他看嗎？

「這個，你剛剛說我可以看看你奶奶的書。」傑可小心地說道。

「是啊，所以呢？」卡特瑞娜說。

「那我可以看嗎？」

「當然可以啊。」卡特瑞娜笑笑地說道，然後從包包裡把那本皮質封面的小本子拿出來，遞給傑可。

當晚，傑可一回到家，就跑進自己的房間裡，掏出那本皮質封面的本子。

你現在知道了，我叫愛蜜麗，這是我的故事。我的父母親在一個以織布業為主的小鎮出生長大，那裡離北英格蘭的紡織重鎮布拉福只有幾哩遠。我父母親結婚之後，就搬到布拉福找工作。

值此之際，正是工業革命發展最巔峰的時刻。布拉福是世界上的毛紡之都，可是生活條件卻很差。大部分都是六個人擠在一個很小的房間裡，紡織廠的大煙囪汩汩地冒出黑煙，污染空氣。河水也受到污染，所以沒有乾淨的飲用水。這裡常常爆發傷寒和霍亂，預期壽命很短。很多兒童夭折，事實上，紡織廠工人的小孩，有三成活不過十五歲。

愛蜜莉

P. 25

工業
・你的家鄉是工業城鎮嗎？或者以前一度是工業區？生產什麼呢？

3. 愛蜜麗

P. 26

我父母親很幸運，1853 年，他們在布拉福外圍幾哩處，一家新的蒸汽發電毛紡織廠找到了工作。紡織廠的老闆提多・索特，他希望改善員工的生活環境，所以就在紡織廠的周圍蓋了一整座小鎮。剛開始，我的父母親是搭火車去上班，後來分配到了一間位於索特爾鎮的房子，那裡也是我度過年少歲月的地方。

我的父親是一位工頭，所以住的房子比其他人要來得大一些些。我們有一間起居室、一間廚房、三間臥室，甚至還有一間蓋在屋外的自用廁所，和一個小小的花園。這個村子四面都是田野，從房子走到運河只需要很短的路程。我們是很幸運的。

P. 27

家庭

- 你知道你的祖父母是從事什麼工作的嗎？那曾祖父母又是做什麼的呢？他們住在哪裡呢？找出答案，在課堂上和大家分享吧。

P. 28

所以現在你知道我生活和工作過的地方囉，我們姑且跳過個幾年不談吧。

1869 年，這一年：俄國大文豪托爾斯泰出版了鉅著《戰爭與和平》，吸塵器發明問世，蘇伊士運河開始通行，而我當時正值十八歲。紡織廠的棉絮被吸進我的肺裡，造成呼吸困難的問題，我所有的朋友也都是這樣。現在還活著的朋友，都算是幸運兒了。露西去年過世了，得年十六。凱蒂在前年去世，當時僅十四歲。所以，看得出來，我算是幸運的了。

不過，生活並不全是惡夢，也會有一些樂趣。星期天時，我們不用上班，我們偶而會去逛布朗＆穆夫商店，那是一家位於布拉福的百貨公司。當然囉，我們只逛不買，猛盯著那些炫目櫥窗中陳列的女裝。衣服的布料是我們製作的，而我們卻買不起衣服穿。有時候逛完街後，我和朋友葛麗絲會沿著運河散一下步。

十二月一個寒冷而晴朗的星期日，我們不小心聽到了別人的一些對話，而這竟成了我們生命的轉捩點。

我們當時就坐在運河的草地岸邊，河上駛過一艘大型平底船，我們能看得見船隻，但船上面的人看不到我們。

P. 29

駕船的兩位舵手一如平常，但奇怪的是船隻停了下來。

「亨利，就是這個地方。」一頭紅髮的高大男子說。

「你確定？」友人問。

「確定。那邊田地上有一輛舊推車，我們可以先把東西放在推車下面，晚上再回來拿。」

他們抬著一個用舊布袋包起來的東西，看起來沉甸甸的，然後走下船。

「你想那是什麼東西？」葛麗絲緊緊抓住我的手臂，小聲問道。

「看起來像是屍體。」我一說罷，她發出了尖叫聲。

兩個男人停下腳步。

「什麼聲音？」名字叫做亨利的男人問道。

「哪知道，搞不好樹叢的後面有人，我們過去確認一下。」紅髮男人說。

葛麗絲的臉變得慘白，我們彼此面面相覷，非常害怕。這時，一隻貓從樹叢下方跳出來，朝著兩個男人衝過去。

「嘿，亨利，沒啥好擔心啦，不過是一隻貓。咱們繼續吧。」

P.30

「傑可，吃晚飯了。」媽媽從樓梯往上喊道。

「好。」傑可大聲回話說。

真是的，才正看到興頭上，很想一口氣看下去，吃飯時間怎麼老是來得不是時候？

有趣

· 為什麼愛蜜麗的故事開始變得有趣？
· 你在讀有趣的故事時，是否有時也會被打斷？
· 是什麼元素在讓故事變得有趣的？

傑可走進飯廳時，大家都已經坐定位了。當傑可走進來時，大家停止了談話。

「不會吧，我有做了什麼事嗎？」他心想。

接著，他看到了叔叔也在場。

4. 傑可

P.31

「傑可，坐下。」父親說：「我們大家先吃飯，吃完飯後，你叔叔有一些事情要跟你談。」

吃完晚餐後，傑可的兄弟姊妹去幫忙洗碗。桑吉特叔叔從口袋裡掏出一張傳單，放在餐桌上。

傑可的心一沉，那是卡特瑞娜的傳單。

「這件事與我無關。」傑可說。

「我知道，但我希望你能夠阻止星期六的抗議行為，你能跟那個女孩談談嗎？她是你學校的同學，對吧？」叔叔說。

「對啊，我已經勸阻過她了，不過她不聽我的。」

「你可以再跟她說一次看看，你知道這家店對我來說是何等的重要。」桑吉特叔叔說：「傳單上講的這些孩子，我的店裡頭沒有賣他們做的衣服。」

「你怎麼知道呢？」傑可問。

「我店裡賣的衣服都是在布拉福這裡生產的，是我一位老朋友在生產的。縫製我賣的衣服的人，我每一個都認識，我可以確定地跟你說，他們沒有一個人的年紀會比你小。」

「那布料是哪裡來的？」傑可問。

「是跟倫敦一個信譽良好的布商拿的。」叔叔回答。

「那麼，布料的棉花又是從哪裡來的？」

叔叔這時露出了不確定的神情，「這我不知道，傑可。」

談話沉默了片刻。

P. 32

「如果你覺得這一點很重要，我可以跟布商問問看，布商今晚會從倫敦過來。」

「太好了，那我會叫卡特瑞娜不要去抗議，但我不能保證什麼。」傑可說。

「謝啦，傑可。」桑吉特叔叔說完，起身準備離開時，又坐了下來。「仔細想想，你何不現在就打電話給卡特瑞娜？我不希望事情是靠碰運氣的。我可是熬了很久的時間，才開了這家店的。」

「我不確定她是不是會過來，叔叔。」傑可咕噥地說道。

「那我們打電話看看就知道了，來吧，現在就打，我晚上還有事要忙。」桑吉特叔叔說。

傑可拿出手機，發了簡訊給卡特瑞娜。

* 我叔叔現在在我家，過來找他，
  他會說明一切。
* 太好啦，你的住址是？
* 王妃街二號

卡特瑞娜早就知道他家的住址，她只是不想讓傑可發現這一點。她隨即關掉筆電，抓了件外套。

「我要去薩米拉家喔。」她大聲跟媽媽喊道。

「別太晚回來喔。」媽媽在門砰一聲關上之際，大聲回話道。

聯絡
- 你通常是如何和朋友聯絡的？是傳簡訊？用 Twitter？用臉書？打電話？傳 email？還是寫信？

5. 桑吉特叔叔

P. 33

卡特瑞娜來到門口，開始感到緊張。她在緊張什麼？緊張要和傑可的叔叔正面交鋒？還是緊張要看到傑可？當然是緊張要和傑可的叔叔交鋒吧，不，其實不然。卡特瑞娜並不害怕和別人交鋒，事實上，她還樂在其中呢。真相是，要看到傑可，才會她忐忑不安。

她用手指頭壓了一下門鈴——五、四、三、二——門打開了，正是傑可。

P. 34

「你真快啊！」傑可說。

「是啊，我們住的地方就差兩條街而已。」卡特瑞娜回答。

「真的嗎？這我還不知道呢。」傑可說。不過，他其實是知道的。

他知道卡特瑞娜的很多事情，也知道她住在哪裡，他只是不想讓她發現而已。

「我們是要整晚站在門口，還是你要請我進你家？」卡特瑞娜問。

傑可笑了笑，往旁邊一站。「不要太難為他喔！」他小聲說道，只讓她聽得

到，「我叔叔他人很好。」

傑可的叔叔這時就坐在長飯桌的一邊，在他面前的桌子上放著一疊卡特瑞娜的傳單。

「叔叔，這是卡特瑞娜。卡特瑞娜，這位是我的桑吉特叔叔。」

「坐下。」桑吉特叔叔說，「這個嘛，如果你不逼我關門大吉，我會雇用你，你很有天分！」他說。

「你在靠童工賺錢。」卡特瑞娜說。

「這你有所不知。」桑吉特叔叔冷靜地說：「你先聽我說，不要急著下結論。」

接著他說明產業的細節，就像他跟傑可說過的一樣。

卡特瑞娜得意地說：「所以，你並不知道在你那些衣服的生產過程中，是不是有雇用童工囉？你有讀過傳單嗎？」她一邊問，一邊指著傳單上講到烏茲別克採集棉花的那段文章：

P.35

「烏茲別克政府表示，『他們國家不允許使用童工採集棉花』，然而《新聞之夜》節目拍攝到一個滿滿都是童工在採集棉花的棉花田。一位男童跟《新聞之夜》說：『我一直要到十一月才會回學校上課。我在這裡每天採集七十公斤的棉花。』另一個男孩說：『我一公斤可以賺兩便士。』有些童工的年紀才九歲大。棉花……」（譯註：一百便士等於一英鎊）

「我知道你的重點了，我同意你的觀點。」桑吉特叔叔插話道：「童工的事情駭人聽聞，我保證今天晚上會跟我的供

應商談這個問題。卡特瑞娜，現在你先跟我說，你畢業後想找什麼樣的工作？」

「我？」卡特瑞娜說：「我想去倫敦經濟學院＊念書。我要讀政治學，以後想從政，要讓童工這種現象從此消失。」（＊註：全名「倫敦政治經濟學院」）（The London School of Economics and Political Science）

P.37

「我知道了，你有偉大的夢想，希望你有一天能夠達成你的夢想。」桑吉特叔叔說：「『去拚拚看吧！』這是我爸以前常對我說的話，『你不會想跟我一樣，一輩子都待在紡織廠裡工作。』他說得沒錯，我並不想。我想擁有一家自己的店，讓人們可以用付得起的價錢買到好的衣服，我也想讓我的朋友來我的店裡工作，最重要的是，我還想自己設計衣服來賣。」

「那你有設計衣服了嗎？」卡特瑞娜問。

「有啊。」桑吉特叔叔回答：「我希望你星期六能夠來我的店，看看我設計的衣服，搞不好你還會喜歡我的設計。卡特瑞娜，你看，這家店就是我的夢想，而且我就快要美夢成真了。」他說：「不要在這時候阻撓我。」

你的偉大夢想

・你畢業之後想做什麼工作？和夥伴討論，並跟全班的同學分享。

「如果你的供應商可以保證棉花的來源沒有問題，我就不會阻撓你。」卡特瑞娜說。

「那就好。」桑吉特叔叔說：「我會先跟他們問清楚這件事情。」之後他看看手錶，「我得走了，供應商再二十分鐘就會到車站了。」

「你要接他們去店裡？」卡特瑞娜問。

P.38

「是，我們要在店裡開會，他們晚上會住在店面樓上的公寓裡。」

「那祝你們順利。」卡特瑞娜說。

緊接著，她發現自己也想去店裡跟著開會，她需要親自在開會現場聽聽看供應商怎麼說。她將椅子往後挪，站起身來。

「我得走了。」她對傑可說。

「你可以多留一會兒啊。」他說。

「不行耶，我要走了，我答應過等一下不會遲到。」

「好吧，那明天學校見啦。」他說道，盡量不露出失望的表情。

「是啊，明天學校見。」卡特瑞娜說。

桑吉特叔叔和卡特瑞娜一起走出房子。

「如果你想，我可以順道開車載你回家。」桑吉特叔叔說。

「不，不用了，我用走的就可以，我就住在轉角那邊而已。」卡特瑞娜說。

他們於是走各自的方向離開。他們兩個人的心裡都在琢磨著要和供應商開會的事情，也都在想著那些在工廠裡超時工作的童工，還有遙遠國度中那些在棉花田打工的童工。

有些孩子應該是在享受童年時光、為未來的人生做準備的時候，但為什麼他們無法像卡特瑞娜或桑吉特叔叔那樣擁有夢想呢？

6. 一捆東西

P.39

卡特瑞娜和桑吉特叔叔身後的門關了起來，現在是七點，要去籃球隊練球太晚了，更何況剛下起雪來了。這時傑可想到了那本小本子。他兩步併一步地走上樓，然後躺上床，拿起皮質封面的小本子，小心地翻到之前看到的地方。

> 「嘿，亨利，沒啥好擔心啦，不過是一隻貓。咱們繼續吧。」
>
> 兩個男人接著穿過田地，抬著一捆人形的東西，朝舊推車走過去。我和葛麗絲目睹他們把那捆東西放在推車下方，然後離去。
>
> 「我們去看一下袋子裡裝的是什麼東西。」我說完便站起來，但朋友葛麗絲又把我拉了下來。

P.40

「你瘋了嗎？」她在我耳邊大聲地耳語道：「我們要等到確定他們已經離開。我跟你說，我想我認得出當中的一個人。」

「哪一個？」我問。

「紅頭髮那個高個子。他是我爸的同事，負責把一捆捆的布扛上船。」葛麗絲說。

「搞不好他們不是只有扛布而已。」我說。

「你這話是什麼意思？」葛麗絲問。

「還扛死人啊。」我說。

「別說傻話。」葛麗絲打哆嗦地說：「你嚇到我了啦。」

兩個男人講話的聲音緩緩飄過田地，向我們這邊傳過來，我們聽到了一些零星的對話，「……今晚，這裡……會付給我們兩先令。」

「他們今天晚上還會再過來。」我興奮地小聲說道。

然後，我們看著那兩個男人穿過田地往上走，翻過最上方的牆。

「走吧，他們現在離開了。我們去看看那是什麼東西。」我一邊說，一邊把手伸向葛麗絲。葛麗絲抓住我的手，我拉著她站起來。

「我們比賽看誰先跑過去。」我說完便跑了起來。

「不要用跑的啦，你知道用跑的話會出問題的。」葛麗絲說。

P.41

我是知道，但我並沒有停下來。天空陽光燦爛，神祕事件又待解決，我當天才不想去管什麼疾病的問題。我跑到舊推車旁，那裡有一捆東西。我想把那捆東西的布袋拉下來，但拉不下來，於是我坐下來，等葛麗絲過來。

「慢吞吞的，來啊！快過來！」我興奮地喊道。

葛麗絲朝推車走過來，然後在我旁邊屈膝跪下來。

「你準備好了嗎？」我說。

「好啦。」葛麗絲說。

我小心地把捆住這包東西的繩子解開，然後合力把布袋往下拉。裡頭並不是人的屍體，而是一捆布罷了。我們兩個人都認得出來，那是薩爾茨紡織廠的布。

「他們偷紡織廠裡的布。」我吃驚地說道。

「我們得舉發。」葛麗絲說。

P. 42

「沒錯，不過時機還未到。我
們晚上再過來，看看要跟他們碰
面的人是誰。」我說。

「我晚上不想再過來了。」葛
麗絲說。

「那我就自己過來。」我說。
我不怕黑啊。

如果你是在紡織廠工作，那
你害怕的會是機器和工頭，他們
比黑夜恐怖多了。我喜歡夜裡的
寧靜，事實上，我之所以喜歡夜
晚，是因為夜晚代表一天工作的
落幕。

於是當晚，我一個人走路回到
運河旁。今晚夜色晴朗，可以看
得到星星。我躲在推車附近的樹
叢堆裡靜待著。

沒等多久，有著一頭紅髮的
男人先出現了。他站在推車旁，
一邊痰咳著，劃破夜晚的寧靜。
之後，另一個男子也走過來了。

我認出了這個男子，心裡不禁一
沉，那是葛麗絲的父親。

「可憐的葛麗絲，我不能去舉
發，那樣葛麗絲的父親就會被抓
去關。她們家會沒有房子住，葛
麗絲會失業，他們會沒有錢，沒
有地方住，然後死去。」我心想。

我望著黑夜，思索著答案。
「我一定得跟什麼人講才行。」
我想。這件事我只能跟一個人
說，那是我唯一能信任的人，那
個人就是詹姆士。

詹姆士的父親是大工頭，「工
頭不會相信我的話，但他可能會
相信他兒子的話。詹姆士愛我，
他會聽我說的。」

P. 44

那兩個男人握了握手。葛麗絲
的父親扛起那捆布，「我上一捆
布賣了五先令，這可是一個月的
薪水啊。這是你的份。」他拿了

兩先令遞給紅髮男子。

「下星期還是同樣的時間。」他嚷道，然後離開消失在黑夜裡。

紅髮男子靠著推車，咳嗽了幾分鐘，然後轉身往反方向離開。

我等了一會兒後，才跑回家。

✻ ✻ ✻ ✻ ✻ ✻ ✻ ✻ ✻ ✻

第二天早上，負責叫醒工人上工的人敲了敲窗戶，大夥兒趕緊起床。現在是五點半，天色還是暗的。我們很快穿好衣服，跑到屋外，進入前往紡織廠上工的人潮。我們沒有吃早餐，八點半才有休息時間用來吃早餐。

一如往常，我和葛麗絲一塊走向紡織廠，這是我們一天中唯一可以聊天的機會。

P.46

「結果怎樣了？」葛麗絲用亢奮的語氣問道，「你有去嗎？」

「有啊，他們偷布，再把布轉賣掉。」我說。

「真的嗎？」葛麗絲震驚地說：「我要跟我爸說這件事！」

「不要，先別說。」我抓住葛麗絲的手腕說道。

「噢，你抓痛我了！」葛麗絲說。

「抱歉，不過你一定不可以跟任何人說，尤其是你爸。」我說。

「為什麼？那個人是我爸的朋

友。」葛麗絲說。

「就是因為這樣，所以才不要跟他透露任何消息，他會很生氣，你也不會想要這樣吧。」我說。

「是沒錯。」葛麗絲說。

葛麗絲不想讓父親起煩惱，他是一位很好的父親，她很愛他。他想給孩子最好的，就算他沒有什麼錢，也都會買小玩意給孩子。

鐘聲響了，六點鐘整，紡織廠的門打開了。

愛蜜麗

• 你想愛蜜麗這樣做對嗎？
• 那你會怎麼做？

P. 47

傑可想到一件事，他停下手邊的閱讀——桑吉特叔叔沒有問過他畢業後想從事什麼工作。沒有人問過他，大家都認定他想當個籃球選手。不過，並非如此。他籃球是打得不錯，而且當然啦，他也很愛打籃球，但這並不是他唯一的喜好。

傑可從床上爬起來，走到書桌旁，打開最上層的抽屜，拿出一本筆記本和一枝筆。他很喜歡畫畫，他並不想當籃球選手，他想當個藝術家。你想想看誰比較酷，大衛・霍克尼還是大衛・貝克漢？奇怪的是，像他這種年紀的人，大都會覺得運動比藝術來得酷。

傑可想去讀藝術學院，這一點他很清楚。他拿起筆，開始作畫。他畫了紡織廠，畫女工們正離開紡織廠，她們走在石階上，往上面的維多利亞路前進。其中有個女孩的臉面向觀者，那是愛蜜麗。但那明明不是愛蜜麗，那張臉很熟悉，那是卡特瑞娜的臉，他在畫的是卡特瑞娜。

P. 48

「卡特瑞娜現在在哪裡？在做什麼呢？」他想。

他想傳簡訊給她，他該這麼做嗎？為什麼不呢？他發了簡訊，之後沒有後悔，起碼還沒有這種感覺。

卡特瑞娜正走向公車站，現在開始下起雪了。

「紛落的白雪就像棉花球，在烏茲別克，棉花球是由童工來採集的——也許這就是一個訊息吧。」卡特瑞娜一邊想著，一邊把外套拉高到耳朵處。她是不相信什麼訊息啦，不過莎蜜拉很信這個，「莎蜜拉也許可以跟我說明這個訊息的意思。」卡特瑞娜心想，笑了笑。

天氣很冷，卡特瑞娜站在公車站等公車，雪這時候下得又大又急。公車來了，她上了車，公車駛離，慢慢朝著市中心前進。

「別太晚回家。」她下車時，公車司機說道，「如果雪一直這麼大，晚一點就沒有公車了。」

P. 49

地面上積滿了雪，卡特瑞娜便用滑行的方式經過了科克中心，接著經過羊毛交易市場，穿過市場大街，那裡是布朗＆穆夫商店在一九七〇年代後期之前的舊址，也是桑吉特叔叔新開張的店的地方。當然，這條街和以前是不同光景，但是建築物都還是一樣。

桑吉特叔叔剛剛跟傑可和卡特瑞娜說，他小時候常常和媽媽來這裡，別的小朋友看的是玩具，但是桑吉特看的都是衣服。

桑吉特叔叔是在一九七〇年代成長的小孩，他那時在櫥窗裡所看到的衣服，是直條紋的全身緊身衣、紫色的小喇叭

褲、矮子樂的鞋子……。在那個時代，什麼設計都很新穎，而且色彩繽紛。

回到一九七○年代，液晶螢幕和磁碟片剛問世，「天空實驗室三號」載著第一隻魚和第一隻蜘蛛上外太空；「ABBA合唱團」的《滑鐵盧》（Waterloo）在英國首度成為暢銷單曲；當時流行的偶像是「海灣搖滾客合唱團」（Bay City Rollers）；受歡迎的電視節目是《警網雙雄》（Starsky and Hutch）；電影的票房冠軍是《火爆浪子》（Grease）；「Pink Floyd合唱團」的《牆上的另一塊磚》（Another Brick In The Wall）是暢銷排行榜冠軍的歌曲；迪斯可天后葛洛莉雅・蓋諾的熱門單曲《我會活下去》（I Will Survive）締造個人新紀錄。

P. 50

這是一九七○年代，桑吉特叔叔也有他的夢想，他想成為一位有名的時裝設計師。

之後，桑吉特叔叔上了倫敦的聖馬汀學院學服裝設計，而當時候布朗＆穆夫商店吹了熄燈號。

布朗＆穆夫商店多年來一直空盪盪的，塵封的大樓，載滿著兩百年的記憶。然而，桑吉特叔叔每一次經過商店舊址時，都會想像裡面滿滿逛街的人正對著他的設計作品讚嘆不已。

他想像著小孩們會停下腳步來盯著櫥窗裡的衣服看，想像做媽媽的這時才找到了自己的小孩布蘭妮啊、潔德啊、阿里啊、娜塔莎啊、潔蜜拉啊、亞碧達等等的。布朗＆穆夫商店以前關閉過好長一段時間，不過卡特瑞娜的媽媽老愛提起這家商店。

一九七○年代

- 你還知道一九七○年代的什麼事情嗎？利用網路來和同學分組討論。

P. 51

卡特瑞娜此時此刻就站在舊址的前面，她抬眼盯著新的店家看板，上面寫著「波希米亞風」（Boho Chic），人們很高興新開了這家店，上面寫著「時髦不用花大錢，耍酷不用多少錢」。

櫥窗隱身在廣告牛皮紙的後面，這已經張貼好幾個星期了，人們很好奇牛皮紙後面究竟藏著什麼。

8. 波希米亞風

P. 52

卡特瑞娜看到對街上停了一輛車子。

「一定是桑吉特叔叔和供應商到了。」她想。

她很快轉身面向商店的窗戶，聽到了被大雪蒙罩住的講話聲，還有轉動鑰匙、打開門的聲音，接著是一片安靜——此刻只剩下她和大雪。

她靜待了一會兒，然後走到大門，想看看門打不打得開。

「太好了，門是開著的。」她心想，然後溜了進去。

房子裡烏漆抹黑的，不過最裡面那一頭的房間裡透出了燈光，卡特瑞娜悄悄地走過去。她躲在靠近辦公室的一個衣架後面，藏身在此處，那些人的談話就可以聽得一清二楚了。他們的聲音迴響很大聲，整個商店裡都可以聽得很清楚。

「你為什麼想知道棉花的來源？這重要嗎？」其中一個叫希德的供應商問。

「是滿重要的，我不想用那些靠童工採集的棉花。現在，跟我說是哪裡來的棉花，不然我就不再跟你進貨。」桑吉特叔叔說。

「可是你很滿意我們的貨啊，品質好，價格又優惠。」亞米爾說。

「是沒錯，這我知道，不過還是請你們跟我說是哪裡進的貨。」桑吉特叔叔堅持地說道。

P.53

「當然是印度來的貨啊，我們的棉花都是跟印度的一家小農場買的。那裡我們去過幾次，我可以跟你保證他們不使用童工。那裡的工人生活條件都不錯，我們很歡迎你自己親自去看看，如果你想，我們可以一起去。」

「好，我有一天會和你一起去參觀那裡的棉花田。你這樣說我就放心啦，我得弄清楚這些棉花不是靠童工去採集。」桑吉特叔叔說。

「這我們了解。」希德說：「如果都沒事了，我想你最好走了，桑吉特，外面的雪下得很大。」

「是啊，你說得沒錯。」桑吉特叔叔說：「這個是樓上公寓的鑰匙，公寓裡什麼都有。我會把車子留在這裡，我不想在這樣的夜裡開車。我會用走的，還滿近的。我車鑰匙也留給你們吧，你們需要移動車子時就可以使用。我們明天早上會從這裡用走的去銀行，我大概九點左右會過來。」

「好，那麼明天一早見。」

「晚安了。」桑吉特叔叔說。

接著，卡特瑞娜看著桑吉特叔叔離開商店。

P.54

「你沒有跟桑吉特說實話。」另一個供應商亞米爾說。

「那又怎樣？他高興，我們高興，大家都高興，這樣就好啦，他不需要知道棉花是從烏茲別克來的。」希德說。

「怎麼可以這樣！可憐的桑吉特叔叔，這些人竟然這樣唬弄他！我現在應該怎麼做？又不能取消這次的抗議行動，因為大部分的棉花可能都是使用童工採集而來的。」

卡特瑞娜的手機這時發出了「叮——叮——」的聲音，是傑可傳簡訊給她。「叮——叮——」，這個聲音又大聲又清楚，在商店裡迴盪起來，聽起來就像警鈴的聲音，而不是手機的聲音。

「喔，不，我怎麼沒把手機關掉？」卡特瑞娜心想。

P.55

「是什麼聲音？」亞米爾問。

「我想是手機的聲音，商店裡還有其他人在。」希德說。

希德跑出辦公室，卡特瑞娜連忙往大門跑去，可惜她跑得不夠快，希德撲過去抓住她的腳，將她拉倒在地。她的頭撞到了地板，心想「哎喲」，接著眼前一片黑暗，頭撞到的疼痛感也瞬間消失。

「我們不能把她留在這裡，她受傷了。」亞米爾驚慌地說道。

「我們不能放她走，我們說的話她都聽到了，她會去跟桑吉特告發，那樣桑吉特就不會跟我們進貨了。我們把她關起

來，來吧，亞米爾，你是這裡的人，我們可以把她藏在哪裡？」希德說。

「好好好，我想一下。」亞米爾說。

店裡頭有個鐘滴滴答答響著，滴——答——滴——答，弄得他緊張兮兮的，無法好好思考。滴——答——，這時，他想到了叔叔的舊船。

「我知道了。」亞米爾說。

9. 遇到麻煩

P.56

傑可繼續讀著日記，一心想知道愛蜜麗的故事會如何收場。

　　詹姆士想娶我，我們想就此遠走高飛——遠離紡織廠，遠離那裡的毛絮和噪音，遠離疲憊、骨頭酸痛和嚴重的咳嗽。

　　我們打算找一間小農舍，地點可能是在湖區，有人跟我們說那裡地勢很高。我們可以在那裡種菜、養綿羊，我想要像我祖母那樣自己織羊毛線。我希望我們的孩子能去上學，這樣他們可以專心念書，不用工作，不要像我們這樣在紡織廠裡長大。

P.57

　　我跟詹姆士說了推車、布和葛麗絲父親的事，他說他想自己親眼來看看，我們就說好當晚在運河那邊碰面。

　　這個晚上，夜空沒有星光，我走過鐵道橋，這時開始下起了大

雪。我來到約好碰面的地方，不過詹姆士還沒有到。雪下得又大又急，「真希望他人趕快出現」，我想。

我等了十五分鐘後，詹姆士還是沒有來。

我不想錯過那兩個人，所以決定自己隻身前往。我沿著運河快步前進，新下的雪地上一路上留著我的腳印。當我來到農田時，那兩個人已經在推車旁了。

我藏身在樹叢裡，然後，接下來發生了一件很慘的事情。我極力想克制住，卻辦不到。我憋住，直到憋不住氣時，我終於咳嗽出來了。

咳嗽聲飄過雪白的田地，傳到推車一方。那兩個人把頭朝我這邊轉過來，知道了有人正在偷看著他們。接著，紅髮男人向我這邊跑過來，我現在知道他的名字了，他叫做湯姆。

我知道我得趕快溜走，可是我跑不動，我人僵住了，可能是凍僵了，也可能是嚇呆了。

我繼續咳嗽著，湯姆這時已經站在我旁邊了。他有六個小孩，其中最大的孩子是我的同事。

P. 58

「你在這裡做什麼？」他帶著驚恐地語氣問道。

「你們在偷竊。」我說。

葛麗絲的父親這時也過來了。「愛蜜麗，你在這裡做什麼？」他吃驚地問。

「我們在幹嘛啊？」湯姆說：「我們不能放她走，她會把事情說出去，那我們的工作和房子就都沒了。」

「葛麗絲知道這件事嗎？」葛麗絲的父親問。

我想了一下，靜靜地說：「知道。」

葛麗絲父親的臉霎時刷白，白得就像我們四周紛落的雪。我為他感到很難過。

「她知道偷布的事，但不知道偷布的人是你。」

「謝天謝地。那還有其他人知道嗎？」葛麗絲的父親問。

我決定說謊。「沒有，只有我和葛麗絲知道。我們上星期沿著運河散步時，看到船停下來，有人抬著一捆布走下船，我們以為那是屍體，所以就一路跟蹤，來到這個推車旁。」我說。

「不能放她回家。」湯姆又說了一次，「我們把她綁起來，讓她今晚留在船上，然後再看接下來要怎麼做。」

「好吧。」葛麗絲的父親說。

我看著他的眼神，我知道他一定不會傷害我，可是對於湯姆我就沒有把握了。

P. 60

我一路靜靜地和兩個男人走回運河那邊，這時候逃跑不是明智之舉，那一天我肺部的狀況很不好，而且又特別的虛弱。

大雪繼續紛飛，運河都結凍了。他們把我帶上船，我們上了船之後不久，葛麗絲的父親就離開回家了，另外那個人——湯姆，他留在船上看守我，我覺得自己小命不保了。

愛蜜麗和卡特瑞娜

• 愛蜜麗和卡特瑞娜都遇到了麻煩，她們的困境有什麼相似的地方嗎？又有什麼不一樣的地方呢？和夥伴討論一下。

事後，我得知詹姆士跑去我家大聲敲門。我父親開了門。

「愛蜜麗在家嗎？」詹姆士上氣不接下氣地問。

「她不在，去葛麗絲家了。」我父親說。

「謝啦。」詹姆士說完，便一路直奔。他知道我不在葛麗絲家，他剛剛才從那裡過來，也知道葛麗絲的父親不在家。他知道我遇到了麻煩，非找到我不可。

他跑過鐵路橋，來到運河旁，在雪地上看到了像是腳印的印子。這不是男人的腳印，太小了。

P.61

「有可能是愛蜜麗的腳印。」詹姆士心想，他決定尋著腳印走。

剛開始時，腳印還算清楚，可是繽紛的雪很快就開始要把整片大地覆蓋住。他尋著腳印走到田地時，出現了很多的腳印，有大有小。

「這裡看起來有發生過衝突。」詹姆士心想，不由得害怕起來。

他朝舊推車直奔過去，看到地上有一捆布，「有人把布扔在這裡，然後匆匆離開。愛蜜麗說得沒錯，有人偷了紡織廠裡的布。」這捆布就是鐵證了。

詹姆士環視了一下四周，然後尋著他看到的三組腳印走回到運河旁。河邊曳船路上的樹木枝頭，積滿了厚重的雪。

詹姆士拼命地奔跑，穿過闃寂的大雪，此時唯一能聽到的聲音，是他砰砰的心跳聲和肺部的喘噓聲。

這時，他聽到了講話的聲音。

他盡全力跑上有五個閘門的那條顛簸小路，接著看到了我。我當時穿著一件緋紅色的外套，披著一頭黑色的長髮散在肩膀上。

那個男人推了我一下，我尖叫了一聲，落在薄冰上，薄冰一個碎裂，我便深深沉入結凍的河裡了。

P. 63

「不！」詹姆士尖叫道，然後沿著路跑上來，在雪地上跌跌撞撞。詹姆士來到船邊後便跳進運河裡，不過他知道太遲了，人掉進結凍的河裡是活不了的。

我在結凍的河裡不斷往下沉，我所有的夢想也跟著下沉。是的，我的夢想，我也是有夢想的，對吧？我說過的。只是，有一個夢想我還沒有透露，我想生一個孩子，而且我不要讓我的孩子在紡織廠工作。不，他還得去學校上課，長大後要去從政，以便拯救那些跟我一樣的孩子。

不過，現在這一切都不過是一場空夢罷了，我不斷不斷地往下沉，帶著我的夢想，沉入冰冷的黑暗之中。

猜猜看

•你想詹姆士有辦法救活愛蜜麗嗎？
•愛蜜麗的夢想是否會和她一起葬在運河裡？和夥伴討論看看，然後與全班同學一起分享想法。

10. 船艇

P. 65

當卡特瑞娜最後醒過來時，她感到渾身又冷又濕。她的頭有個地方好痛，她還聽到一個很清楚的聲音，那是運河船隻「卜──卜──卜──」的聲音。她人怎麼會在運河上？她最近記得的一件事情，是她去找傑可，「接下來呢？女孩，趕快想想看！」

接著，她恢復記憶，心臟也開始加速。

「商店──桑吉特叔叔──那兩個人，他們要把我帶去哪裡呢？」她開始想像各種情況，「他們要把我丟進運河裡，戲碼在重新上映，歷史在重演，他們要把我丟進運河裡，就像那個人對我曾曾祖母所做的事一樣。」卡特瑞娜心想，「這裡可能是索爾泰爾的運河，事情會不會太巧合了？莎蜜拉不會這樣想，莎蜜拉會說這是注定好的命運。」

這時，突然傳來河水快速流動的洪聲，「天啊，船在下沉！」

卡特瑞娜大聲尖叫，不過叫聲被水聲蓋過去了。水灌進來，但船並未下沉，這時她忽然想到，「現在我知道是怎麼一回事了，我們在水閘。」她心想，不由得鬆了一口氣。這時，她有一個想法，「我來算算水閘，那樣就可以知道我們的位置了。」

P.66

卡特瑞娜開始算，「有五個水閘！全國只有一個地方有五個水閘，我知道我們在哪裡了。」

「卜——卜——卜——」，引擎聲這時候停了下來，船也停了下來。她聽到有人拴住船，接著是離去的腳步聲。

「他們會再回來嗎？我有多少時間可以逃跑？」她心想著。

她的左腳被一個鍊子拴住，跟著門鎖在一起，她無法逃脫。她的手雖然沒有被綑住，卻也無計可施。

接著，卡特瑞娜感覺到放在口袋裡的手機。

「我可以發簡訊給傑可，跟他說我在哪裡，他會知道要怎麼做的。」她很快從口袋裡掏出手機，打簡訊道：

P.67

　＊我在運河的船上，五……

就在這時，卡特瑞娜聽到一個說話聲，整個害怕起來。船晃動了起來，像是有人踏上了船。卡特瑞娜很驚惶，「現在就要把簡訊送出去。」她想。當她按著發送鍵時，手都在發抖。只希望傑可能讀出她人在哪裡。接著，她又躺了下來，閉上眼睛。這時她能聽到船另一頭的說話聲。

P.68

「你要去檢查一下那個女孩嗎？」一個聲音說道。

「不用，她插翅難飛——她的腳上拴著鐵鍊！況且，她人還在昏迷中，她的頭撞得很大力。我們到底打算要怎麼對付

她？」

「我還不確定。」希德說：「我們可以讓她和船一起沉了。」

「你是在開玩笑的，對吧」亞米爾驚嚇地問。

「也許是，也許不是！」希德笑笑地說，「不過，有一件事是可以確定的，在桑吉特付清棉料的錢之前，她是哪裡都別想去。到時候，等我們拿到錢了，我們再潛回倫敦。」

「然後把她留在這裡，讓她在又冷又濕中死掉？」亞米爾驚嚇地把話說完。

「是誰說要讓她死的？你驚悚片看太多啦。」希德拍拍亞米爾的背，說道。

「拜託，傑可，求求你，傑可，你一定要看懂我的簡訊啊。」卡特瑞娜躺在黑暗裡，小聲地不斷對自己說。

卡特瑞娜沒有回簡訊。十分鐘過去了，她還是沒有回。

傑可在記事本上塗鴉，半個鐘頭過去了，還是沒回。

他繼續畫著，「她大概是不想回我的簡訊吧。」

他又畫了更多的畫，「會不會是出了什麼事？但是從我家走到她家，能出什麼事呢？」

P.69

傑可在房裡踱起步來，「她會不會是沒回家，而是去跟蹤我叔叔了？」

一個鐘頭過去……兩個鐘頭過去……

「叮——叮——」，傑可的手機上閃出了卡特瑞娜的名字，傳進來了一個簡訊：

＊我在運河的船上，五……

五什麼？她是什麼意思？我沒去過運河，看不懂她的意思。是五座橋嗎？還是五個鎮？五什麼呢？傑可需要幫助，他隨即打簡訊給他的死黨賽門：

「盡快在索爾泰爾運河和我碰面，卡特瑞娜遇到麻煩了。」

但是賽門又不認識卡特瑞娜，傑可於是把她的名字刪除掉，改寫成：

「我有麻煩了，請看這個：我在運河的船上，五……。你想是五什麼呢？見面時跟我說。」

「叮——叮——」，「我上路了，五什麼？我想想。」

這則簡訊還打上了一個微笑。傑可抓起外套穿上，然後把日記塞進口袋裡。他不知道自己為什麼要帶上日記，搞不好裡頭會有線索，可以幫忙找到卡特瑞娜。

一到了屋外，他解開自行車的鎖，騎了上去。現在雪已經停了，不過地面上的積雪還是很厚。傑可全力踩著腳踏車，駛過安靜的銀色世界，腦子裡盤旋著「五」這個數字。

當傑可來到索爾泰爾時，賽門已經站在鐵路橋等他了。

P.71

「五」——紡織廠在運河邊，也許卡特瑞娜指的是五個紡織廠的窗戶，或是五個煙囪，哪裡有五個煙囪？傑可也不清楚。

他猛力剎住車，腳踏車在斜坡上往下滑，濺得四處都是雪，最後在賽門的前面停了下來。

「不賴嘛！你怎麼這麼久？」

「又不是每個人的昂貴腳踏車都有二十檔變速器外加雪地專用輪胎。」傑可說。

「是啊，沒錯，但願如此。」

「你有想到『五』代表什麼了嗎？」傑可問。

「搞不好。你呢？」賽門問。

「沒有，不過我想應該是和紡織廠有關係，就這麼覺得。」傑可一邊說道，一邊把手伸進口袋，用冰冷的手指緊握那本皮質封面的小本子。

「我不這麼想，運河上只有一個和『五』有關的東西，那就是五個水閘。」

「當然，卡特瑞娜的人就在那裡。」傑可說。

「卡特瑞娜？她是誰？她和這些有什麼關係？」

「卡特瑞娜？」傑可說：「嗯……卡特瑞娜就是那個動員星期六要去我叔叔店門口抗議的女生。」

「喔，我想起來了，就是那個你今天下午在練習籃球時急急忙忙跑去找的女生。」賽門說。

「對，就是她。」傑可一邊說，一邊看著地上，右腳踢著雪。

「我還是搞不懂。」賽門說。

P.72

「是她遇到麻煩，不是我。我是說真的，她真的有麻煩了。」

賽門本來想揶揄一下朋友，不過這時看到了傑可的眼神裡有著恐懼。

「五水閘離這裡多遠？」傑可問。

「騎快一點的話，十或十五分鐘可以到。」賽門跨上腳踏車，「走吧，我們來比賽看誰先到。」

在積雪的曳船路上騎腳踏車是很吃力的，不過傑可毅然決然地上路，而且很快就遠遠地把賽門甩在後面。

他一來到五水閘的地方便下了車，把腳踏車扔在陡坡的下方，然後用跑的爬

上坡，在雪地上跌跌撞撞。他看到上面栓了一艘舊船，最後拚命跑了幾公尺，來到了船的正對面。

P.73

傑可查看了一下船，看到了卡特瑞娜的臉正朝著一個窗口壓過來，而卡特瑞娜也看到他了。

「這裡沒有其他人，他們把我丟在這裡。」她喊道。

傑可在她的眼神裡看到恐懼，看著她張嘴閉嘴，但是聽不清楚她在說什麼。

他跑過橋，來到運河的另一邊，跳上船，水濺了起來！傑可驚恐地往下看，他的腳邊淹水了。

「船要沉了，我們沒有太多時間了。」他說。

「我知道。他們把掛鎖的鑰匙留在廚房，這是他們說的。他們說他們並不想讓我死，只是不想讓我去跟你叔叔告密。」卡特瑞娜說。

「是誰？是誰做的？」傑可。

「傑可，現在沒有時間講這些，我之後再跟你說。去找掛鎖的鑰匙，要在船下沉之前逃出去。」

「他們把船弄破一個洞，想害死你，他們是殺人犯。」傑可說。

「我想船不是他們弄破的，是因為船太舊的關係。快去找鑰匙吧。」卡特瑞娜說。

傑可走到廚房，鑰匙就放在水槽旁邊，一眼就可以看到。「卡特瑞娜說的可能是對的，他們大概不致於要讓她死。」傑可心想。

P.74

傑可很快拿起鑰匙，走回來想打開掛鎖，但是掛鎖因為太舊了，怎樣也打不開鎖。他看看下面的水，水已經淹到腳踝了。

「水灌進來得很快，我們一定要趕快出去。」他想。

賽門這時也來了。「傑可，你還可以嗎？你那邊需要我幫什麼忙嗎？」

「你不要上船，這樣會讓船身下沉得更快。」傑可焦急地大聲喊道：「快去叫救護車！」

傑可的手指又僵硬又冰冷，而且抖個不停。他心裡很害怕，但是他不想讓卡特瑞娜看出來。

「我要是打不開掛鎖，怎麼辦？」他想：「我不能把卡特瑞娜一個人丟在這裡，我一定要跟她身邊，一起死掉，對，就這樣。不過這不會發生的，我們一定可以逃出船，這又不是鐵達尼號，對吧？而且這裡也不是在大海上，這裡是利茲·利物蒲運河。」

他又轉著鑰匙，這一次掛鎖打開了。

「我打開了！」他說道，然後抱了一下卡特瑞娜，之後兩人不禁尷尬地互視了一下。

「謝啦。」她靜靜地說，「我還以為無望了。」

這時，船的前端突然往前下沉。

「快，我們要趕緊出去。」傑可大聲喊道。

賽門站在曳船路上，神情很緊張。他幫他們拉出船。之後他們一邊等著救護車前來，一邊站在那裡目睹船沉入河裡。

P.75

傑可把手探進口袋裡，口袋裡什麼也沒有。

「日記──我把日記弄丟了！」傑可心想：「我把它放在外套的口袋裡，可是現在不見了，這下子我就不知道愛蜜麗接下來的發展了，而且，我要怎麼跟卡特瑞娜交代呢？那本日記是她的寶貝啊。」

救護車嗡嗡作響，閃爍著警示燈，救護車終於到來。醫護人員朝著他們跑過來，傑可也把日記的事拋在腦後了。

11. 愛蜜麗的夢想

P.76

星期六早上，陽光燦爛，卡特瑞娜和朋友們沿著街道，一路往「波希米亞風」前進。他們都很興奮，也有一點點緊張，每個人的手上都拿著一疊傳單。

「所以，我們真的要去發傳單了。」莎蜜拉説。

「當然啦，這件事我忙了那麼久，才不想現在半途而廢呢。你們不會緊張吧？」卡特瑞娜説。

「有一點，我以前沒做過這種事。」莎蜜拉説。

「沒事的。」卡特瑞拉勾了一下莎蜜拉的手臂説。

他們一路上開心地邊走邊聊天。

「再跟我們説一次那天晚上發生了什麼事情。」莎蜜拉央求道。

「你説是傑可來搭救你的，哇，真是好運耶！」海倫娜説。

P.77

傑可和桑吉特叔叔這時正站在「波希米亞風」的階梯上等著他們到來。商店樹窗的牛皮紙已經拿下來了，人人都能看到樹窗裡的陳列。

「哇，商店看起來好棒啊！」卡特瑞娜説。

「謝謝你們前來。」桑吉特叔叔説：「也謝謝你們寫的宣傳單。」

「是傑可幫我的，上面的插畫都是他畫的。」卡特瑞娜説。

「我知道，他人很好，不是嗎？」接著他面向其他人説：「就這樣沒錯，現在大

119

家都站好位置了。不可以聊天喔，你們是來這裡打工的。要聊天等一下再去咖啡廳聊。」

「是的，讀者們，你猜中了，我取消了抗議活動，我們來這裡不是來發抗議傳單的，而是來幫『波希米亞風』發廣告單的。不過，你們還是不知道愛蜜麗後來怎樣了，對吧？這我待會兒再跟你們說。我先說一下『波希米亞風』的現況吧。桑吉特叔叔後來找了一些新的供應商，而他們的棉花千真萬確是從印度一個小農場買進來的。你知道嗎，桑吉特叔叔還說暑假時要帶我去參觀那邊的棉花田喔。而希德和亞米爾，他們的審判下個月就會出來了，這件事讓我很緊繃，我現在不想多想。想當然耳了，店今天能開張，就是一件很成功的事。桑吉特叔叔設計的衣服很讚喔，我的朋友都這麼說啦，我也認同。」

P.78

商店打烊之後，卡特瑞娜和傑可一起在商店的咖啡廳喝東西，一邊等著桑吉特叔叔和其他員工結完現金帳。

「卡特瑞娜，我有件事情一定要跟你說。」傑可說。

正在喝飲料的卡特瑞娜抬起頭，傑可一臉正經的樣子。

「什麼事？」卡特瑞娜不安地問。

「我從運河船上把你救出來的那個晚上，我隨身帶上了日記，而我……」，他停下來看著卡特瑞娜。

「怎樣？」卡特瑞娜問。

「我把它弄丟了。」傑可難過地說道。

「你要說的就是這個？」卡特瑞娜鬆了一口氣地問。

「這麼說，你不生我的氣？」

「不會啦，我早就把整本日記都打進我的筆電裡了，所以日記的內容都還在。」

「既然如此，你可以告訴我故事最後的結局嗎？我還沒看完，很想知道愛蜜麗最後怎樣了，她有死掉嗎？」

「她不可能死掉的啊，對吧？她要是死了，就不會有我啊，不是嗎？笨蛋！」卡特瑞娜說完便笑了起來，接著又一臉嚴肅地說：「愛蜜麗沒有死，但是她最後也沒有得到童話故事般的結局。」

「她有跟詹姆士結婚嗎？」

「有，他們結婚了，不過他們沒有搬去湖區，而是留在索爾泰爾。她後來也生了一個兒子，不過兒子沒有上大學，也沒有去從政，而是在紡織廠裡工作。」

「那麼說，她的夢想就要由你來完成囉。」

「是啊，很有趣吧。但願我可以。」卡特瑞娜說。

ANSWER KEY

Before Reading

Page 6

1

a. theft, kidnapping, romance
b. in the past and the present

2

a. The story in the present.
b. With marriage and children.
c. With a dream coming true.

Page 7

3

a. Emily
b. Caterina
c. Emily
d. Emily
e. Caterina
f. Caterina

Page 8

4

a. Industrial
b. polluted
c. terrible
d. better
e. healthier
f. educational
g. cheaper
h. local
i. huge
j. great

Page 9

6

a. towpath
b. lock
c. canal bank
d. barge
e. canal

7

a. canal
b. canal bank, barge
c. towpath
d. lock

Page 10

8

a. 5
b. 7
c. 6
d. 2
e. 3
f. 1
g. 4
h. 8

9

a. 2
b. 5
c. 3
d. 6
e. 4
f. 1

10
a. A leather book.
b. A roll of cloth.

Page 11

11
a. Designing the clothes.
b. Choosing the material to make
the clothes.
c. Making the clothes.
d. Selling the clothes.

Page 60

They were both discovered by
the people they are watching, are
kidnapped and put on a barge.
Emily is still conscious; Caterina is
unconscious.

After Reading

Page 81

a. T
b. F
c. F
d. T
e. F
f. T
g. F

2
b. She was her great-great grandmother.
c. They worked in a mill.
e. She was afraid of Tom.
g. James managed to save her.

3
a. steam-powered woolen
b. overlooker
c. breathing
d. dead body
e. little treats
f. footprints
g. five locks

Page 82

4
a. 3
b. 5
c. 1
d. 6
e. 2
f. 4
g. 10
h. 9
i. 8

5

a. Jake's
b. Caterina
c. Uncle Sanjit
d. The suppliers: Sid and Aamir
e. Aamir's
f. Simon
g. Jake

Page 83

1

determined, brave, ambitious, kind, impulsive

Page 84

4

a. great-great grandmother
b. 1851
c. easy
d. school
e. eight years old
f. Lake District
g. children like her
h. mill

Page 85

5

a. 2
b. 3
c. 1
d. 3
e. 2
f. 4
g. 4
h. 1

Page 86

1

a. 2
b. 3
c. 1
d. 4
e. 2

Page 87

3

a. d. e. f.

4

(Caterina)
a. 2
b. 1
c. 5
d. 4
e. 3

(Emily)
a. 4
b. 2
c. 1
d. 5
e. 3

Page 88

1

a. cheap
b. chesty
c. trendy
d. flared
e. polluted
f. icy

2

a. flared trousers
b. chesty cough
c. polluted river
d. cheap scarves
e. trendy clothes
f. icy water

3

a. 9
b. 8
c. 6

d. 1
e. 2
f. 3
g. 10
h. 7
i. 5
j. 4

4
a. was published
b. started
c. opened/was opened
d. wrote
e. was invented
f. carried
g. was recorded
h. was

5 Possible answers
a. *Wuthering Heights* was published in 1847.
b. The iPhone was invented by Apple.
c. The first laptops appeared in the early 1980s.
d. *Pride and Prejudice* was first published in 1813.
e. The television became commercially available in the 1920s.

After Reading

Page 90

1
a. T
b. F
c. T
d. F
e. F
f. F
g. F
h. F
i. T
j. F
k. F
l. F
m. T
n. F
o. T

Page 91

2
b. They were noisy and unsafe.
d. She thought it was terrible because of child labor.
e. He asked his suppliers and wanted to make sure there was no child labor involved.
f. She went to Uncle Sanjit's shop.
g. They looked at the window displays.
h. Emily didn't tell her.
j. Grace's father left her with Tom.
k. She counted the five locks.
l. He asked Simon for help.
n. They both managed to save them.

3
a. 2
b. 4
c. 4
d. 1
e. 4
f. 2

125

國家圖書館出版品預行編目資料

英倫女孩站出來 / Elspeth Rawstron 著 ; 安卡斯
譯. —初版. —[臺北市] : 寂天文化, 2013.10　面
; 公分.

中英對照
ISBN 978-986-318-143-9 (25K平裝附光碟片)
1.英語　2.讀本

805.18　　　　　　　　　　102016003

作者 _ Elspeth Rawstron
譯者 _ 安卡斯
校對 _ 陳慧莉
封面設計 _ 蔡怡柔
封面完稿 _ 郭瀞暄
製程管理 _ 宋建文
出版者 _ 寂天文化事業股份有限公司
電話 _ +886-2-2365-9739
傳真 _ +886-2-2365-9835
網址 _ www.icosmos.com.tw
讀者服務 _ onlineservice@icosmos.com.tw
出版日期 _ 2013年10月 初版一刷（250101）
郵撥帳號 _ 1998620-0 寂天文化事業股份有限公司
訂購金額600（含）元以上郵資免費
訂購金額600元以下者，請外加郵資65元
若有破損，請寄回更換

〔限台灣銷售〕